Angels
of
Defense

Chris Copeland

SOLE PUBLISHING LLC
Paperback Edition

Chris Copeland

Angels of Defense

ISBN: 0-615-21806-7

EAN-13: 978-0-615-21806-9

Printed in the United States of America

Published by Sole Publishing, 52 Eaton Rd., Tylertown, Ms 39667

Paperback Edition

Book 2
of the

Kastle Law Series

Castle Doctrine-The state of Florida in the United States became the first to enact the Castle Doctrine (or Castle Law) on October 1, 2005. The Florida statute allows the use of deadly force when a person reasonably believes it necessary to prevent the commission of a "forcible felony." Under the statute, forcible felonies include "treason; murder; manslaughter; carjacking; home-invasion robbery; kidnapping; aircraft piracy; unlawful throwing, placing, or discharging of a destructive device or bomb, and other felony which involves the use or threat of physical force or violence against any individual."

On October 1, 2005, the Castle Law was passed in the state of Florida. The following events lead to its creation.

Chapter 1
Rally Cap

"Can I get you anything else, Mr. Raines?"

"I believe we're all set. Thank you Becky," I said to our young, attractive waitress.

"I wouldn't stand too close to him, he likes giving 'good games'," Mason stated.

"He's kidding," I said to Becky. I was pretty sure that she knew that I would not touch her backside, but I wanted to make sure.

"I wouldn't care, but I'm sure his wife would," Becky replied.

"He used to play baseball," Mason said, as he attempted to explain his comment to Becky.

"Did you play for the Marlins?" She asked. Rocco and I were in there regularly and we had talked to her many times before. She knew that we had a private security business, but we had never discussed anything about our past.

"No, I didn't make it that far," I replied.

"Did you have any superstitions?" She asked.

"No, I have never been that superstitious," I answered. "

"My boyfriend was telling me about some pitcher the other day that would bite off the tip of one of his fingernails for luck and kept it in his mouth the entire game," Becky explained.

"That's crazy," Rocco responded.

"No, I never did anything like that," I said.

"I need to check on another table, but let me know if you guys need anything," Becky said.

"Thank you, Becky," I said. She placed the check on the table and left the outside balcony.

"Now, you can tell us the truth. I know you had some kind of superstition," Dante said.

"There has to be something," Mason added.

"No, really there's nothing worth mentioning." I paused for a second and then smiled. "There was one guy, my rookie year, in Great Falls, Rick Carter. He was a superstitious nut. He believed in witchcraft and everything else. Some of the guys wanted to have some fun, so they bought him a hooker. At the end of the night, they gave her instructions to give him a fake number when he asked for it. A week later, they got the same girl to meet up with us, at a bar, after a game. She went home with him. When they were done, she pulled out one of his pubes and burned it with a lighter. She told him that she put a spell on him and he was cursed. From that moment forward, he would be madly in love with every Pam that he came in contact with. The only way for him to not be in love, was by plucking a pubic hair from each one he encountered and burning it."

"Why did she use her name?" Rocco asked.

"Pam was the team owner's wife," I answered.

"Was this you?" Dante asked.

"No! I chipped in for the second hooker. I had to see if he would do it. We gave the girl heads up of what would happen and paid her extra," I explained.

"Did he do it?" Mason asked.

"Yeah," I responded.

"What happened with the owner's wife?" Rocco asked.

"I came clean, before he got to her. He told me that he had plucked three others, besides the hooker. I felt bad; he was Maced twice and took three stitches from an alarm clock," I said, as we all laughed.

"He deserved what he got," Rocco replied.

When we finished our breakfast, I slid the check across the table and positioned it between the plates of Dante and Mason. I pulled my hand back, grabbing my glass of pineapple juice on the way. I took a sip and looked out over the beach. I took a moment and savored the presence of my closest friends. In that instant, I felt normal. We were four regular guys, just eating breakfast to start our day. It felt good. It was a diverse table. Rocco, a proud Italian-American, was seated to my right. Mason, a black, Italian-American, was seated beside him.

Dante and I completed the circle with plain, old, black and white.

In the previous seven months, I had been expecting something bad to happen. We followed up on everything that I was told in New York and it all checked out. Still, there was a part of me that was not totally convinced. I guess part of it was that I enjoyed doing something for a cause that I believed in and I did not want it to be over. It took seven months, but I was gradually embracing reality and my upcoming challenge of fatherhood.

Dante and Mason had been down for the weekend, and were returning to Jacksonville after breakfast. We were seated at a secluded table on the second floor balcony of the Overlay Restaurant that overlooked South Beach in Miami. The food there is excellent; breakfast, lunch, and dinner. Plus, the view is magnificent.

"We are regulars here, so make sure Becky is well taken care of," Rocco said playfully, glaring at Mason and Dante. They lost the bet on our golf game and had to pay for our meals over the weekend.

"Whoa! You, of all people, can't say that we don't tip well," Mason said, while turning up his hands.

"Haven't you seen us throw money around all weekend?" Dante added.

"I'm just saying that you are not as generous as we are," Rocco replied.

"Before Kastle showed up, you were the tightest person I had ever met; don't try to deny it. You would break out the calculator whenever you picked up the check. He even had his on percentages that he went by. Great service was given an eleven percent gratuity, but his standard was seven," Mason said, as we all laughed, including Rocco.

"I'm more generous these days, but I've never carried around a calculator...and eleven percent may be the lowest that I've ever given," Rocco responded.

"I think seven percent sounds more like it," Dante said.

"Believe what you want!" Rocco responded. He turned and looked at Mason. "You've been quite the comedian this weekend."

"I've missed you bro!" Mason replied.

"So, how's business?" Dante asked.

"Business is good. The loss of Rush hurt; but, we have some new prospects that Tristan has referred to us," I replied.

"With Tristan Lake on the roster, you know we are all good. Rush's absence is irrelevant," Rocco said.

"What's the latest on Rush? Will he see any time?" Dante asked.

"He's facing ten years for gun charges. I don't know any details. He's no longer a client," I replied.

"We had to cut loose the dead weight," Rocco added.

"What was he thinking?" Mason asked.

"He's a dumbass!" Rocco stated.

"We shouldn't be too quick to judge without hearing his side of the story. How about innocent until proven guilty," Dante responded, clearly defending his favorite rapper.

"He bought a dozen AK-47's from an ATF agent. He's fucked!" Rocco replied.

"Well, if that's the case, he's done," Dante said.

"Oh, it's true," Rocco replied, as we were finishing off our breakfast.

"I've been meaning to ask you...How do you like your new toy? You haven't been in it all weekend," Mason said to me.

"I love it," I answered with a huge smile on my face. I had always wanted a Ferrari for as long as I can remember. I finally got a F430 a week before the guys came down.

"It's a beauty! You can't go wrong with an Italian sports car," Rocco added.

"Did you get it okayed by Gus?" Dante asked.

"Of course! It's okay to spend money, as long as we're careful. You can't take it with you," I stated.

"Why are you giving Kastle a hard time? You have a new Bentley sitting in the garage," Mason said.

"Did Gus sign off on it?" Rocco asked.

"Trust me, I always follow protocol," Dante answered, with his patented mischievous grin.

"Gus had better be keeping you two in line. Now is not the time, to have any government agency investigating us," Rocco stated.

"Chill, underboss! Everything is all good. Gus's contacts have informed him that we have nothing to worry about. We have no enemies," Dante replied.

"I don't want to be investigated at all. Life is good and I want it to stay that way," Rocco said.

"Are you guys ready?" I asked, as I was looking at a new text message from Bianca. She informed me that Comcast was sending someone to the house to fix a problem with the cable and I needed to be there. I was looking forward to kicking back and watching the Dodgers/Giants game, which was coming on later that afternoon.

"Yeah. We better get going; we don't want to be late for our flight," Mason replied, as he and Dante took care of the bill. Afterwards, we got up from the table and walked toward the exit.

"What are you doing this morning that is so important that you can't ride with your boys to the airport? Do you have to get a five hundred-dollar haircut?" Dante inquired.

"No haircut; I have to let the cable guy in and I need be at home when Bianca returns from her doctor's visit," I answered.

"There's enough time for you to see us off," Dante stated.

"When your beautiful wife is carrying your child and she gives you a simple chore to do, you do it," I responded, as we were walking toward the stairs.

"I wouldn't know anything about that," Dante replied.

"Me neither. How is Bianca doing? I've always heard that pregnant women become a different breed," Mason said.

"She's doing great. There have been mood changes, but nothing crazy," I replied.

"When is her due date?" Dante asked.

"October fourteenth," I answered.

"Three weeks! Boy, the time has flown by," Mason replied.

"It has," I responded. I reached the bottom of the stairs and stepped onto the first level of the restaurant. Rocco and the guys were behind me, casually strolling toward the front door.

"Is it a boy or a girl?" Dante asked.

"We were supposed to find out today, but we decided to wait and be surprised," I said to the guys, who were all looking at me.

"I'm happy for you," Dante replied.

"We all are," Mason added.

"How's that leg doing?" Dante asked Rocco. Rocco was still limping from banging his knee, when he wiped out on a jet ski over the weekend.

"I'm okay. It's just bruised," Rocco replied.

"You might need to get that checked out. A knee injury should be treated sooner rather than later," Mason stated.

"I'll see how it feels in a day or so, but I'm sure it'll be fine," Rocco said. We now made our way to the sidewalk outside of the restaurant. I, immediately, recognized that there was a group of people blocking the path to our cars.

"What do we have here?" Mason said, quickly dropping his conversation with Rocco.

While walking, I noticed a police car parked directly across the street from our vehicles. There was a small crowd in front of the Armed Forces

Recruiting office, which was not too far from our vehicles. They were closer to Rocco's white Cadillac Escalade that was parked in front of Bianca's new black Range Rover. I drove it to the restaurant and Bianca rode with Isabella, Rocco's wife, to her doctor's visit.

"You guys are empty handed; where are the signs that you were suppose to bring?" A tall, slender black guy, wearing a plain white t-shirt, said as we were approaching them. He looked very familiar, but I couldn't immediately remember who he was. The group of eight was all young: late teens and early twenties.

"I have a sign for you." Rocco replied.

"Shouldn't ya'll be in class or something?" Dante asked, as we were now standing in front of them with our backs to the Armed Forces building.

A smaller white kid, wearing a red trucker hat, answered, "We're getting extra credit for attending a rally and writing a report on it. If we make the news, we can replace any test grade with an A."

"And this is what you came up with, a protest against the war?" Rocco said.

"Na man, we support the troops. The man, in there, raped a friend of ours," the black guy explained, as he pointed at a white man, in his late twenties, with a high and tight haircut. The man had a smirk on his face, as he stared out the window at what was going on in front of him.

"He has made her life hell. So, we decided to make him miserable for a day," the guy in the trucker hat said.

13

"I read about that. She was a freshman wasn't she?" I replied.

"Yep," a couple of the guys in the crowd responded.

"What about innocent until proven guilty? You shouldn't be too quick to judge," Dante stated.

"Where there's smoke, there's fire," I replied.

"Uh-huh!" Mason said.

"If it's true, he should be strung up by his nuts!" Rocco shouted, which made everyone in the crowd laugh.

"All I'm saying is…wait until after the trial, before you crucify the guy. Who knows how reliable this girl is," Dante said.

"I do! She's telling the truth," the guy in the trucker hat said.

"If he's guilty, he disgraced the uniform. They can do whatever with him," Dante responded.

"You guys are in the military aren't you?" The black guy said, looking at Dante and Mason.

"Ex-military," Dante responded.

"Come on, you guys have a flight to catch," I said to Dante and Mason, as another guy was, walking toward us, carrying a few colorful signs.

"Here we go," the guy in the trucker hat said, as he grabbed a sign that read, "soldiers are rapists."

"We have a little time," Mason said with a grin.

"If you raise that sign up, it's going up your ass!" Rocco said, raising his voice considerably.

"Yeah, this is what we need. When we kick your asses we'll definitely be on the news," the trucker hat guy said, though he still had his florescent green sign down by his side.

"You don't want that," Mason replied.

"You must be the muscle of the group," the trucker hat guy stated.

"Whoa big man, we don't want any trouble. We're just here for extra credit," the black guy said in a respectful manner or at least it seemed that it was his intention. "You don't want to mess with these dudes; soldiers go looking for a fight," he said to his friend.

"Now, there's someone with common sense. The rest of you should fall in behind this one," Rocco replied.

"We're getting hungry out here. Why don't you go and get us something, pizza man?" The punk in the trucker hat said, as he and the other guys in the crowd began to chuckle. Dante quickly grabbed a hold of Rocco after the kid's remark.

"You little bitch!" Rocco shouted.

"Pepperoni with extra cheese!" The trucker hat guy blurted out the insult, looking away from Rocco and avoiding eye contact from any of us.

"I'll chunk you through that plate glass window!" Rocco angrily replied, while pointing at the recruiting office.

"What do you say we take him in the alley and throw a blanket party for him," Dante suggested to Rocco.

"Don't you mean block party?" The trucker hat guy stated.

15

"He's an idiot. Why are we wasting our time with this?" Dante said, as my eyes were fixed on a kid that was standing in the crowd. He was squinting his eyes and staring at Rocco. While I was looking at him, I noticed something being passed around that eventually ended up in the hands of the tall black guy. Moments later, another kid walked up to him holding a medium sized wooden stick with the American Flag attached to it. The black guy opened his right hand and a black lighter, with a white skull on it, became visible. I instantly snatched it from him.

"If your reflexes were better, you wouldn't have dropped those two passes on Saturday," I said, as I finally realizing who he was; thus, generating a slight grin from him.

"I caught five passes for eighty-five yards and the winning touchdown!" He replied, quickly defending his performance.

"Andre Mayo; you had a nice game the other day. You seem pretty smart. All it would take is one incident, like this, to get you in trouble," Dante added.

"Then, there'll be no football; but I'm sure you can find a good rally to fill the void," Mason said.

"Dre! Don't listen to these old guys. There'll be no incident. The toy cops over there are here for show; they aren't worried about us. They're busy flirting with the counter girl at Coffee Ville," the guy in the trucker hat said.

"That's where you guys should be," Dante added.

"Jeff, ease up, these guys are alright. Let's get out of here," Andre said to the guy in the hat, as he started to walk away from us, attempting to get the rest of the group to follow.

"They're punks! What color panties are your wife wearing? I'm thinking either, red or green," Jeff said to Rocco.

"Oh, that's your ass," Rocco replied, as Jeff went up to the kid that was holding the flag.

"No!" Andre shouted. Jeff put the flame from the lighter near the flag. We all rushed toward him. Rocco was the first one there. He grabbed Jeff and slammed him on the hood of a white, new model, Chevy Malibu that was parked in front of Rocco's Escalade; and boy did he slam him! Instantaneously, everyone scattered in all directions. Rocco and the guys jumped into his Escalade; while, I grabbed Andre and urged him to come with me. He accepted my offer and dragged his, dazed, buddy along with him. He put Jeff in the back seat and jumped in the front. Momentarily, we were in my Range Rover and leaving the scene, following closely behind Rocco. The two cops were frantically running around, trying to stop someone; but, from what we saw, they had no success. I thought about doing the responsible thing and stop, but I didn't. No one was harmed, so I felt that nothing would be achieved if we stuck around. My cell phone rang a few seconds later, with Rocco's name appearing on the screen.

"Who's with you?" Rocco asked.

"Who do you think?" I answered.

"Do you need a hand with that? I would be more than happy to give that little prick a ride to wherever he needs to go," Rocco said.

"I have it under control. I'm giving them a ride to campus. Are you headed to the airport?" I replied, while glancing at my passengers.

"...As quick as possible. These two are magnets for trouble," Rocco said.

"I'll call you later," I said, as Rocco turned right and we continued straight ahead.

"Was that the one who jumped me? Follow him; I owe him a beating," Jeff said, as he leaned forward between the front seats.

"It's funny that you waited until he got off the phone to say something," Andre replied.

"I was being polite," Jeff responded.

"Sit back! You're not going to do shit, which is a good thing. These guys are not people you want to mess with. You could wake up in the morning and have a shark head next to you in your bed," Andre said.

"You catch on quick," I said, glancing over at him.

"I got to be; to keep my boys out of trouble. See, we have something in common," Andre replied.

"We do," I said.

"Dre, why are you kissing this dude's ass? You are losing cool points by the second," Jeff said sarcastically, from the back seat. I turned and looked at him for a second, then looked back at the road.

"Tonight, go to Orso and ask for Stan. He will have your name on the VIP list. No lines and no stamp on your hand," I said, as I looked at him in the rearview mirror. Jeff had a faded black star, with a white "O" in the middle that was stamped on his right hand, obviously from the night before.

"Oh, you saw my stamp. I'm not going to waste my time. Only celebrities set foot in VIP," Jeff replied. The Orso Lounge is a hot spot on South Beach that is labeled as an upper echelon establishment on the bar scene. It is always packed and there is always a line.

"He knows somebody. What do you do?" Andre asked.

"I know the owner. I have clients that go there quite a bit and he wants that to continue," I answered.

"What kind of clients?" Jeff asked.

"All kinds," I responded.

"Why, so secretive?" Andre asked.

"Why, so many questions?" I replied.

"I guess I wasn't too far off with the shark head comment," Andre said.

"Creative, but no; it's nothing like that," I said, shaking my head, while I handed him my card.

"Kastle Raines! Is this your security company?" Andre asked, as he was looking down at the card.

"He can't protect shit! Who are some of your clients?" Jeff asked.

"Tristan Lake, and others," I replied.

"Who else do you work for, that we would know?" Andre asked.

"Rushon Little was a client, until he was arrested," I answered.

"See, if you were doing your job, your clients wouldn't have to arm themselves with automatic weapons," Jeff said, as I rolled my eyes.

"Do you want to be on the list or not?" I responded, while I was turning the steering wheel. We were now on the campus of the University of Miami.

"Hell yeah, but on Friday; it sucks on Monday night," Jeff replied.

"Okay, be there Friday night," I said.

"Don't make me regret doing this. Stay out of trouble," I responded.

"We will! You have my word," Andre replied.

"We'll be on our best behavior," Jeff added.

"Go two more blocks and take a left; you can drop us off at the dorm on the right," Andre explained. We arrived in front of their dorm and they began to get out. "We appreciate the ride," Andre said, as he was opening the door.

"No problem. Take care," I said, as he closed the door and they walked toward their dorm. I made my way off campus and headed to my house.

Chapter 2
The Other Shoe

On the way home, I stopped in at a gas station to pick up a few things. I went inside and retrieved a six pack of Bud Light from the cooler and a pack of Altoids, which was on a rack beside the register. I paid for everything and exited the store. After taking a couple of steps, a man, sitting in his truck, hitting the steering wheel, immediately grabbed my attention. The man noticed me and drooped his head down in embarrassment, as I continued toward my car. He got out of his ninety-something model Silverado, which was parked beside a gas pump, and came in my direction. I stopped immediately and stood beside a car that was parked next to mine.

"Excuse me!" The man said, while walking toward me.

"Yes," I replied, as I popped an Altoid in my mouth.

"So I guess you saw that?" He asked.

"Don't sweat it, I get pissed like that all the time," I answered, just as he made it to me, now only a few feet away from each other. He was a man, in his mid to late twenties, wearing coveralls with splattered white paint on them and white, what was once brown, work boots.

"This is really hard for me to ask and I wouldn't, if this wasn't important. I'm doing a job not too far from here and I have to get home to take my wife to her checkup. They don't take checks here and my gas and credit cards are maxed out. I just need a few dollars to get me home. The baby will be here in less than a month and we have been buying a lot stuff to get ready for it. My wife's car went into the shop on Friday, just to top everything off. If you could spare a few dollars, I would really appreciate it," the man said.

"I can help you," I replied, as I went into my wallet.

"Thank you, I promise I will send you double what you give me or you can follow me home," he said in a desperate tone.

"That won't be necessary; but, I will take a card if you have one," I replied.

"Of course! Here you go," the man said, as he handed me his card.

"If I come across any work for you, I will definitely send them your way," I stated.

"My wife's car is almost identical to yours. Have you had any problems with it?" He asked, while pointing at the older model, Nissan Altima that we were standing beside.

"That's me over there," I said, pointing at our Range Rover and momentarily, handing him a hundred dollar bill.

"I only need a few bucks, let me go in and get change for this," He replied. He took a step toward the entrance of the store.

"I don't want any change. It is all yours," I stated. He immediately stopped and turned toward me.

"This is too much. I can't accept this," He said, as he tried to give it back to me.

"Please, consider it as a baby shower gift," I responded.

"What is your name?" He asked me after a few seconds of silence, with a look of appreciation clearly visible on his face.

"Kastle Raines," I answered.

"I owe you. If you ever need anything, please call," he said.

"I will, it was very nice to meet you," I said, as I began to walk away.

"Thanks again," he said, as he turned and went toward his truck. I saw him pumping gas in my rear view, as I drove away. At first, I was skeptical about the truthfulness of his explanation, but as he continued talking, he sounded genuine.

I arrived at home, maybe ten minutes later. I put the beer in the fridge and waited for the cable guy to arrive.

"Hello, are you Kastle Raines?" A man said, as I opened the door. He had short, dark hair and a goatee. He was Hispanic and he was wearing blue coveralls, which had a white emblem of his cable company, Comcast, on his right front pocket. The name "Juan" was in white letters, on the left side of his coveralls and he was carrying a clipboard in his left hand.

"Yes I am," I replied.

"I have a work order for a repair to your cable box," he explained.

"Yes, please come in," I said, as I opened the door all the way and let him in.

"You have a very nice home," Juan responded.

"Thank you, the box is over there," I said, as I followed him into the living room. He started working and I went into the kitchen.

"Can I get you anything to drink?" I asked.

"Water would be great. It has been a busy morning," Juan replied, as he walked toward the kitchen. I grabbed a bottled water from the counter.

"Here you go," I said, as I set the bottle on the bar in front of him, where he immediately removed the top and took a sip.

"Thank you!" he replied.

"Do you know what the problem is?" I asked.

"The cable going to the outside box was cut," he responded, while he set his bottled water on the countertop. My eyes lit up, as he was bringing his right hand from the bottle. It looked as if it had been severely burned and there was a tan line on his middle finger from a ring or a piece of string. He noticed my reaction and immediately cracked a disturbing smile. I countered by cracking his nose, which sent him staggering backwards with blood gushing from both nostrils. I quickly made my way over to him and punched him in his left jaw numerous times, which knocked him to the floor. I was not carrying a gun on me at the time, but I did have a 9mm stashed under the middle cushion of the couch, that I quickly got to. (I had a couple of them stashed in various rooms of the house. Rocco turned me on to this practice with the same setup at his house.) He made it to his feet, but I quickly sent him back down with a blow to his chin. I rapidly went to him and put my gun against his head.

"You surprised me. Where I'm from, this would never happen to me," he said, after he momentarily gathered himself.

"Welcome to America. What name are you going by these days?" I asked him.

"You know my name," he replied.

"Zane Cotto," I replied, as I pressed the barrel of my gun against his head.

"Whoa! Don't do it. I have to come out of here...or your wife and her friend are dead," he said.

"What?" I said, as I gritted my teeth.

"My people have not touched her yet. If they don't get a call from me soon, then they'll grab her and...you know what will happen next," he replied.

"You're bluffing," I stated.

"It's true. Do you think I would come in here without an exit strategy? Your wife is my ticket out of here." He was right; there was no way that I was going to let him just walk out. "Family and friends are liabilities. That is one of the advantages I have over you. Because of you and your associates, I don't have any weaknesses," he stated, as I took a step back from him.

"Where's your gun?" I asked.

"I don't have one."

"Put your hands behind your head and interlock your fingers!" I demanded.

"I underestimated you; I see that my brothers never stood a chance," he replied, while he was following my instructions to the "T." "Especially Ponce, he was the weakest. He had a soft spot for Americans. The other two were loyal soldiers, but they were sold out by your friend Adam. I put their deaths all on him. I have searched for him for months, but he has disappeared off the face of the earth. Something tells me I have you to thank for that. I take it you were told that Adam Marshall was really me. I had that put out there to keep me off your radar," he said, sitting on the floor, with a gun pointed at his head.

"I've waited for this for a long time," I said.

"You and your people have cost me a lot of money; for that, you will pay," Zane said, using a stern voice.

"Is that so?" I replied.

"Your wife, her friend, and your unborn son will be safe, when I walk out of here. As for the rest of America, no one is safe!" Zane forcefully said. I was stunned when he said, "unborn son," but I didn't want to show it. I backed up from Zane and let him up, glancing down at bloody knuckles on my right hand. I grabbed the gun with my left hand and kept it pointed in his direction. I made a fist with my right hand and grimaced; the adrenaline was beginning to wear off.

"You have my attention," I replied, as he sat down in the chair next to the couch. I remained standing, with my gun down by my side.

"You Americans hate to lose. I will make you pay by killing many people and you not being able to stop me. Everything's already set in motion. Stop me if you can," Zane said with a smile.

"Why come and tell me this? Why not just do it?" I asked.

"That would be too easy. I want you and your friends to pay for killing my brothers. This will be the biggest attack that your country has ever seen. Are you up for the challenge or are you scared?" Zane said.

"You're sick! I should just end this now with a bullet to your head," I retorted.

"It's an addiction. There's nothing like blowing up a building that has stood for decades. The sound of the blast, the piles of rubble covering dead bodies, all provide a feeling of satisfaction that is unmatched. The fear, by all, that follows in the aftermath is the ultimate high and the reason that I must do it, over and over again," Zane Cotto said, giving me a disturbing glimpse of inside his head.

"I was wrong; you should be tortured and then a bullet to the head," I replied.

"I want you to know how much I want this…to give you more of an incentive to stop me. I am competitive, just like you," he said. The more he spoke, the more I could see that he was educated.

"I thought all of you people had a finger missing?" I asked, after glancing at both of his hands. In the past, I had heard stories about him and his brothers.

"I was the only one who was spared. I was dowsed with acid instead," he replied. I took a second look at his right hand. If what he said was true, it was the first time that I had ever seen the after effects of acid on the skin. It was hideous and definitely was not something I cared to see again.

"All of that is unfortunate, but this country had no part in any of that. So where does your hatred come from?" I asked.

"I've been programmed, by years of torture, to not like you," he answered.

"I don't like you either. It's you, who has changed our lives forever. I will make sure that you get what you have coming to you," I said, as I raised my gun and pointed it at him; with my left hand I pulled my cell phone from my pocket and took a picture of him sitting in the chair.

"You won't find any information on me anywhere; I don't exist," he stated, while I was sending his picture to Rocco's phone. "This has been fun, but if I'm not out of here in a few minutes; your family will die," he said.

"If I was to let you go, how do I know that they'll be safe?" I asked.

"I'm telling you that they will. I have no intent in hurting them, as long as I'm able to walk out that door. From there, I will disappear," he stated.

"What is your challenge?" I asked, with my gun still by my side.

"You have to prevent a one day massacre; with no help from the authorities. If you get help, you and your friends' families, will be killed. None of you can stop this from happening, all you can do is keep your family safe," he said.

"You must underestimate us?" I asked.

"Never! This is why you will only get minor details. There are three bombs, three destinations, and three hundred thousand casualties that you have to worry about. I don't have enough time to tell you about the day that will be remembered forever, but I'm sure you can figure out all you need to know. I'm giving you more than enough time for you to do so."

"How much time would that be?"

"It could be days or weeks. Time shouldn't be a problem for a competitor like you. But, don't forget; any help from cops, then your friends and families are dead," Zane said. He rose up from the chair. I wanted to pull the trigger and be done with it, but I had to go with my gut feeling and let him leave. It was one of the hardest things that I ever had to do. "Well, this is goodbye. Good luck! This will be fun," Zane said, with a cocky smile permanently planted on his face that made me want to smack him.

"We'll meet again," I said, while he went to the front door and opened it.

"I hope so. I love challenges," Zane said, as he continued to smile when he walked away from me. A few seconds later, he started the van and drove off. I immediately called Rocco on my cell, while I shut the door and hurried back inside.

"Why are you sending me pictures of guys?"

"It's Zane, fucking, Cotto!" I yelled into the phone.

"No! You're fucking with me," Rocco asked, as I sprinted to my office.

"No! He was just in my living room. I had a gun to his head, but I had to let him go. He told me that he had men following Bianca and Isabella, and would kill them if he didn't come out alive. I was able to stick a tracking device on him. Is Dante and Mason still with you?" I said, talking very fast. I kept a small tracking device on my gun; it was like a small, clear piece of tape. I slipped it in Zane's back pocket, as he was getting up from the living room floor.

"No, they just took off!" Rocco replied, while I was opening a locked box that contained the tracking device receiver.

"Get them back and I'll call you when I'm on the road. Get some of our guys to pick up the girls, wherever they are. I'll see if Gus can find out how Cotto will be leaving the country," I said.

"What did the cocksucker want? ...To kill you?" Rocco asked.

"Not just me...I'll tell you everything, later. Let me go," I replied, while running through the house and out the door.

"Okay!" Rocco said, as we hung up. I wasted a few extra seconds by going into the garage and getting the Ferrari, but I planned to make it up. I jumped into the silver F430 and began my pursuit. I pulled out of the driveway; then, gassed on it, and oh did I feel the horses. I had a lot of ground to make up, so I really opened her up. I went as fast as I could, weaving in and out of traffic. I used the tracking device to point me in the right direction. I was now on 42nd Avenue, about three miles behind him, when I received a call.

"Hey beautiful," I said.

"What is going on?" Bianca replied.

"Are you okay?" I asked.

"Yes! Why are we supposed to stay here and wait for someone to come and get us?" Bianca said.

"Has anything happened out of the ordinary?" I replied.

"...Other than this? No! I haven't been around anyone other than Isabella and my doctor," Bianca stated.

"Good! We have to take care of something, but we're sending someone to bring you to me," I said.

"You still haven't answered me, why?" Bianca said, while sounding very annoyed.

"I can't get into it right now. I'll explain everything soon. I have to go. I love you," I said.

"Be careful! I love you too," Bianca said, as we both hung up our phones. I set my sights on the task at hand, still driving northwest on 42nd Avenue. After ten minutes, I had cut the interval between us in half. I continued in pursuit, making phone calls along the way.

"Kastle, I'm on vacation. All business can wait until we get back from Paris," Gus said, upon answering the phone.

"Where are you?" I asked.

"I'm at the airport, with my beautiful bride, waiting for our flight," Gus answered.

"We need you down here! We have an emergency! I'm chasing Zane Cotto as we speak. He has big plans that we have to stop," I said.

"Are you sure it's him?" Gus asked.

"Yes! We had a nice conversation in my house ten minutes ago," I replied.

"What happened?" Gus asked.

"I had a gun on him, but I had to let him go. His men were in place to grab Bianca and Isabella, if I didn't. I was able to put a tracking device on him and I am in pursuit. I need to know how he'll be leaving the country," I said to Gus.

"It will be a while before I can have any intel for you, but I will do what I can," Gus replied.

"Okay, I'll see you when you get here," I said.

"I'm on the way," Gus said, as we both hung up our phones. I continued on, glancing at the flashing red dot every so often. At the twelve minute mark, it stopped moving. Once I got within a mile, it started up again. I assumed that he had stopped to switch cars. Moments later, Zane turned onto the Dolphin Expressway heading east. Meanwhile, I called Nate to see if he could get the information I needed. He takes care of things when Rocco and I are out of the office.

"Hey boss, the wives have been picked and they are safe," Nate said.

"That's great news; I appreciate it. I need one more thing. I need to know every flight or ship that is leaving the Miami area in the next couple of hours. Check all cities in south Florida," I said.

"Do you have a destination in mind?" Nate asked.

"Anywhere south of Florida," I answered.

"Okay, I'll get back to you when I find something." Nate said.

"Thank you!" I said before hanging up.

"Rocco, where are you? I'm on the Dolphin Expressway, closing in on Zane," I said, as I looked down at the blinking dot.

"I have the boys and we are on the way," Rocco said.

"I think he's going to the Port of Miami," I replied.

"I know a shortcut; we can be there in five minutes," Rocco stated.

"You will beat us there. Do you have any guns?" I asked.

"Yes, do you?" he replied.

"I do," I answered, with the Port Boulevard Exit now visible up ahead.

"We'll park and be ready for Zane to arrive," Rocco said.

"Okay, see you in a few minutes," I replied. I hung up my phone and exited off the expressway. I believed that Zane was now in a taxi cab. (There was limited traffic; therefore, making it fairly easy to positively identify the vehicle that I was tracking.) The taxi reached Port Boulevard, while I followed at a safe distance. I phoned Rocco to give him an exact location.

"The cab is about to stop at Pier 5 and there is no one in the vicinity," Rocco said, as soon as he answered his phone.

"Take him down when the door opens; I will block the cab," I stated, as I was coming up on Pier 5. I immediately located the cab about a hundred yards ahead. I could see the guys moving in, which prompted me to slam on the gas. I arrived there in a matter of seconds, sliding to a stop in front of the cab. The passenger side door was only a foot away from the front bumper of the taxi. I saw a surprised taxi driver, as I put my SUV in park. I grabbed my gun and exited my car. I ran around the back and joined the guys at the cab. I drew my gun and approached the driver's door.

"Keep your hands on the steering wheel!" I yelled, as Rocco opened the driver's door; while Mason and Dante were jerking Zane out of the back seat of the cab. They slammed him to the pavement, which pleased me very much. Rocco pulled the driver out as I had my gun pointed at the driver.

"Kastle! This isn't him," Mason yelled.

"What?" I shouted. "See what he knows," I said to Rocco. I ran to the other side of the car where Dante and Mason were standing over a man that was sitting on the ground about five feet from the car. "Fuck!" I yelled out, after seeing the terrified black man.

"I knew it wouldn't take long," Mason said, after my outburst.

"Who are you?" Dante asked.

"My name is Sam Lewis." It was obvious that he was scared shitless and it seemed that he had not been in situations like this too often. He was in his thirties, medium height, and medium build. Mason grabbed his wallet from his back pocket and tossed it to me. I opened it and verified that he was, who he said he was.

"Why are you here?" I asked, as Dante searched the back seat of the cab.

"I work on that boat over there," the man responded.

"Where are you coming from?" Mason asked.

"We've been here for a few days. I dropped off a rental car and caught this cab here," the man replied, talking very fast. Dante reappeared from the cab with the blue coveralls in his left hand and a black bag that he placed on the ground.

"Where did you find that?" I asked.

"They were stuffed underneath the driver's seat," Dante replied, as I checked the back pocket and found the tracking device.

"What's in here?" I said, looking down at the bag.

"Let's see," Dante replied, as he bent down and began to unzip the bag.

"Wait!" The man said, as he made a sudden move toward the bag.

"Hold up, Sammy!" Mason said, as he snatched the man back, by his right arm, to his original spot.

"Who are yaw? Cops? I want to see some I.D.! ...Show me a warrant while you're at it," Sam said, getting louder and louder. He took another step toward the bag.

"Calm down!" Mason shouted, after he jerked him back again.

"We are looking for the person who was wearing these. Can you help us?" I said, as I held up the coveralls.

"I have no idea. I didn't see who was in there before me," he said. We all were curious to see what was in the bag after his reaction.

Dante resumed unzipping the bag, after getting sidetracked from Mason snatching up Sammy. He opened the bag wide and we all leaned in to get a peak. We saw a variety of baggies filled with pills, weed, coke, and other party favors that he must have needed for the high seas.

"So, that's what you want; go ahead and take it," Sammy said.

"We don't want your stash," I said.

"This is a lot of weight," Mason stated.

"He's a small-time dealer," Dante added.

"I am an entrepreneur. People have needs when they're out for days at a time. I'm just looking out for my co-workers," Sammy said, as Rocco and the cab driver was walking up to us.

"He picked up our guy two miles from your house and dropped him off at Crowne Plaza on 42nd Avenue. He was last seen boarding an airport shuttle bus. There was no small talk or any information given. He gave the driver a bill for his trouble and he had no bags or a ticket that was visible. Seconds later, the driver picked up this one at a rental car place next to the hotel and drove him here," Rocco informed us. After hearing that, I immediately called Nate.

"What's up boss?" Nate answered.

"I need to know where all of the flights that have left Miami in the past hour are going. Call me back!" I said.

"You got it," Nate replied, as we hung up.

"We're sorry for the inconvenience; but believe me, it was necessary. Here's a little something for your hold up. Do you have a card or a number that we can have in case we need a cab?" I said, as I handed him two hundred dollars.

"I don't want any trouble," the cab driver replied.

"Neither do we. Come with me, I'll explain it," Rocco said, as he escorted the driver to the other side of the car.

"Come with me," I said to Sam, as I lifted up the black bag and carried it to the sidewalk. Dante and Mason followed close behind, escorting Sammy. I set the bag down on the sidewalk at the feet of Sammy. "This is your property, we don't want it. There may come a day when you can help us. We have your information. If you are ever contacted, you will be expected to do everything in your power to help us. Agreed?" I said to Sammy.

"Agreed," he replied, as he picked up his bag. "Who are you guys?" He asked, after a long pause.

"You are free to go," Mason responded.

"You have a lot of coveted items in there. Leave before we change our mind," Dante added.

"I'm gone!" Sammy said, as he hurried away with his bag at his side. Rocco made his way to us, while we watched Sammy walk away.

"Zane Cotto is a slippery fuck," Rocco said, upon arrival.

"Fuck! I should have killed him," I stated.

"You had no choice, you couldn't whack him. It would've been too messy. You would have been pinched for sure," Rocco said.

"We'll get 'em," Dante replied.

"Yeah, but for now we have a bigger problem to worry about. Zane has given us a challenge. We have to stop a number of bombings and save three hundred thousand people," I explained.

"Are you sure that he is telling the truth?" Rocco asked.

"I think so. Why else would he risk showing himself? Either way, we have to check it out. Let's go, we have a lot of work to do," I said, as we walked toward our cars. Mason went with Rocco and Dante rode with me. We headed to my house to regroup and plan our next move.

Chapter 3
Clients in low Places

"Tristan, what's up buddy?" I said, answering my cell. Dante and I were on our way back to my house, when my phone rang. We were following Rocco and Mason, who were directly in front of us.

"How are you?" Tristan asked. He was back in L.A., taking some down time before his next project. I usually talk to him at least once a week; he has become one of my closest friends over the past seven months. We talked the day before, so I knew that there was a particular reason for his call.

"It has been a weird day," I replied.

"How so?"

"I have actually been busy today. I had a nice relaxing day all planned, but there were some business stuff that came up that I have to take care of," I stated.

"Business is actually the reason I'm calling. Rush called me and wanted some advice. You're the only person I know that may be able to help him. I know his contract with you guys was terminated; but, could you speak with him, as a favor to me. He has a rather convincing explanation for his situation," Tristan said.

"I would, but I'm in the middle of something at the moment," I replied.

"You know I wouldn't ask, if I didn't think that it was important. Our boy Rush is really freaking out. Talk to him and see if you know where he needs to take the information that he has," Tristan said.

"What information?" I asked.

"I'll let him tell you; if it is true, I don't want to be connected to any of it," Tristan answered.

"That's smart," I responded.

"What can I say? You've rubbed off on me. It's a little late, but Rush is being careful as well. He called my agency, which transferred the call to me and he used his manager's brother's phone. Something is up," Tristan stated.

"Okay, I'm curious. I don't have much time, but I will stop by. Can I speak with him now?" I asked.

"Yeah, he'll be at home. He's working nonstop, until he's locked up," Tristan answered.

"Okay, I'm on my way. I'll talk to you later," I said.

"Hey, I really appreciate this. I owe you one," Tristan replied.

"Yep! I'll talk to you soon," I said.

"Later," Tristan said. Our conversation ended and I immediately dialed Rocco to inform him of what I was doing.

"Yeah," Rocco said.

"I have to make a stop and check on something for Tristan. You guys go ahead and go to my house. Call Gus and see when he's getting in," I said.

"I'll send a car for him, when he arrives. What are you doing for Tristan?" Rocco asked.

"Just a favor; it shouldn't take too long. I'll fill you in when we get home," I said.

"Okay, see you then," Rocco replied. I hung up my cell and we headed to Rushon Little's estate.

"What's the deal?" Dante asked.

"We're going to talk with Rush. He came to Tristan with something and I agreed to hear him out," I explained.

"Do we have time for this?" Dante asked.

"There's nothing that we can do about Zane, until we hear something from Gus. Let's see what Rush has to say. We won't be long," I replied.

We made it to Rush's Mansion about fifteen minutes later. Rush met us at his front door and invited us in.

"Kastle, it's good to see you. I appreciate you stopping by," Rush said, as he greeted us.

"Rushon Little...Dante Jackson," I said, as I introduced them. "He's one of my closest friends," I said to Rush, while shaking his hand.

"It's a pleasure, I'm a big fan," Dante said, extending his hand.

"Hello, it's very nice to meet you," Rush replied, as they shook hands.

"It's good to see that you have a little color in your organization now. Is he one of your soldiers?" Rush asked.

"No, I own a security firm in Jacksonville," Dante responded.

"Even better! Would you like something to drink? I have Powerade," Rush said, while we were walking to his refrigerator. As soon as we stepped in his house, we heard music playing. The instrumental version of a song, which I had never heard before, was coming from small speakers that were in each room.

"That's fine," I replied, as Rush tossed Dante and I a Powerade.

"Thank you," Dante said, upon reception.

"What's this music?" I asked.

"Will this be on your album?" Dante asked.

"No, I'm working on a track for a movie. I like to walk around and feel the music, then the lyrics will come," Rush stated.

"We don't want to hold you up, so let's get to it. You know our policy is to have all personal guns registered through us. We do this, so our clients will avoid problems with the authorities," I said.

"There wasn't enough time for that. I had to protect myself," Rush replied.

"I understand that, but you should have come to us first with any security issues that you had," I responded.

"I know, but it all happened so fast," Rush said.

"What happened?" Dante asked.

"What is with the secrecy that Tristan was telling me about?" I asked.

"I'm being careful; because I'm pretty sure my phone is bugged."

"Why do you think that?" I asked.

"A few months ago, I was in the back room working on the album in my studio. There were three of us back there laying down a track, when five guys walked in that I'd never seen before. There were three Latinos tatted up and carrying guns; an older Latino, in his mid forties, with a scar under his bottom lip who wasn't strapped and none of them ever said a word. The guy with the scar just stood in the background and observed. The ring leader was Latin-American in his thirties that was more American than Latino, but looked like he had a mixture of other nationalities. He had short dark hair and a goatee. He stood out in front of the others, with no gun, and did all of the talking," Rush said.

"Were you or your boys strapped?" Dante asked.

"No. I had a registered 9mm by my bed, which you guys have record of, but not in the studio. Anyway, the guy asked me how the album was coming and when would it be released. I told him it would be released in October and he said that he wanted to give me money. He was giving me a hundred thousand dollars to put a few words in my first single," Rush said.

"What were the words?" Dante asked.

"The first day of October," Rush replied.

"How did the verse go?" Dante asked.

"'The return of the boom on the first day of October, smoke a shroom, bounce until you're sober.' Haven't you heard it on the radio?" Rush asked.

"Of course! You might not be a client anymore, but I'm still a fan," I replied.

"Did you take the money?" Dante asked.

"I told him no, then he had his tatted-up Latino hood rats, grab my boy and put a gun to his head. I didn't think a few words would hurt anything, so I told him I would do it. He said, the money was in an offshore account that he would transfer in two days when he visited me again to hear the song. He handed me a piece of paper that had me and my family's bank account numbers on it. He said if I didn't do this or if I went to the cops, then there would be millions placed in these accounts to throw up red flags and then the accounts would be emptied."

"Who came up with 'the return of the boom'?" I inquired.

"I added that…it's the title of my album?" Rush replied.

"What happened next?" I asked, very intrigued at what he had to say.

"The next morning I got a call from my mother. She received a dozen black roses from me. After I hung up with her, he calls and says that he just wanted to get my attention, and would see me the following night. That night, we go and buy guns. The next night he doesn't show, he just calls. He gives me the offshore account number over the phone and said that I had two hours to bring the track to a radio station and let them play it. He said that he would call back to see which station and if it was played, he would never bother me again. My man at 99 Jamz played it at nine o' clock. At eleven, I had cops searching the house because of an anonymous tip. I told them the truth, but all they could see was a high profile bust," Rush said, as we listened attentively.

"I thought an undercover sold you the guns?" Dante asked.

"The media reported that, but the D.A. hasn't told me or my lawyer that," Rush replied.

"Did you see if his hands had been burned?" I asked.

"I don't know. There were guns pointed at me. At the time, I was worried about self preservation," Rush replied.

"Would you recognize him, if you saw him again?" I asked.

"The motherfucker is taking years away from me, hell yes I remember him," Rush responded, while I reached in my pocket and took out my phone.

"Is this him?" I asked.

"Yes! Who the fuck is that?" Rush replied loudly.

"A future 'number one,' on the 'ten most wanted list'," I responded.

"You don't know his name?" Rush asked.

"Zane Cotto," I answered.

"You're kidding? I knew his brother, but I never saw him. In fact, I've never heard of anyone ever seeing him; it is almost like he doesn't exist. I only heard stories about Zane Cotto," Rush said.

"It sounds like he has a big problem with you," Dante replied.

"Yeah, but I don't know why. I've gone out of my way to distance myself from the past. I've seen his brother several times over the years and he was cool with me. Believe me, if he or his brothers have a problem, they deal with it," Rush said.

"Which brother did you see?" I asked.

"Ponce is the only Cotto that I ever met. I liked him," Rush answered.

"It looks like Zane feels a little different. Has he contacted you since you were arrested?" Dante said.

"No, he hasn't, but I would love to be locked in the Octagon with his bitch ass," Rush responded.

"Do you have that offshore account number?" I asked.

"Yeah, I'll get it for you," Rush replied.

"I know some people who may be able to help you. I believe you, but they will want to check your story out before you will be cleared of the charges," I said.

"You're in good hands," Dante added.

"So, are we working together again?" Rush asked.

"It looks that way. We'll have a new contract for you to sign in a day or two. There will be a security detail assigned to your home. Until your trouble blows over, you need to stay here," I stated.

"Okay, I'll do whatever you say. I just want all of this shit to be over with," Rush replied.

"We'll do our best to make that happen," Dante said.

"We have to go, but I'll be in touch," I said, as Rush gave Dante and I a fist bump.

"I really appreciate this. I'll see ya," Rush replied, before we left his home. We returned to my car and got back on the road.

"You know Zane believes that Rush gave us information on his brothers and he is making him pay for their deaths," Dante stated, as we were leaving Rush's driveway.

"That's part of it, but his main objective was to get the date to us," I replied.

"He might have given him the wrong date to throw us off track," Dante responded.

"Maybe, but I don't think so. This is a big fucking game to him and he wants information out there to make this more competitive. It'll be up to us to find it," I said.

"Well, at least now we have the date," Dante replied.

"Yes we do," I responded.

Chapter 4
Double Trouble

"Hey pretty lady," I said, as Bianca was walking toward me. Isabella followed her in, closed the door behind them and eventually made her way to Rocco in the kitchen. (Dante and I had just arrived a few minutes before. We were in the living room looking for anything that Zane might have left behind, when our wives walked in. Dante joined Mason and the others in the kitchen, as Bianca was approaching me.)

"Oh Kastle!" Bianca said, bursting into tears, as she came into my arms.

"It's okay," I replied, and then gave her a kiss on her forehead.

"Obviously it's not, if I need a bodyguard to go to the gynecologist," she responded, after pulling back from me. "...And if there's blood on my carpet," Bianca said, after she spotted a small blood stain beside the couch.

"I'm sorry, but it couldn't be helped. Everything is fine now," I replied.

"No it's not and I want to know the whole truth; but, there's something I want to tell you first," Bianca said.

"Okay, what is it?"

"I slipped up and found out the sex," Bianca said, as she put her hand on her belly.

"What? I thought we were going to wait," I replied.

"You always know everything! For once, I just wanted to know something before you did," she said.

I grabbed both of her hands and held them. "I slipped up too. I'm sorry baby. I know it's a boy and I'm so happy."

"I can't believe that you don't know," she said, as her smile got even bigger.

"What?"

"We're having a boy...and a girl," she said, which absolutely shocked me. I was definitely not expecting that.

"What?" I said, as the news was still registering.

"We're having twins!" She happily informed me.

"Twins!" I said, as we hugged and we both were ecstatic. I was glad that Zane was misinformed. I enjoyed being surprised and I wanted to share this special moment with Bianca.

"I can't believe I pulled it off," she said.

"So after every visit, when you stayed behind to talk with the doctor, you were checking on the other baby?" I asked.

"Yes I was. I'm sorry for deceiving you," she said.

"You got me," I said with a big smile. "How are they doing?" I asked Bianca, looking at her stomach.

"They are amazing. Everything is going great. In fact, I have something for you," Bianca said, as she handed me a picture.

"Wow," I said, looking down at a sonogram of my babies, with my right arm wrapped securely around my beautiful wife.

"It is called a 3D sonogram; isn't it incredible," she said.

"Yes it is," I replied, staring down at it. I couldn't take my eyes off of it, it was truly remarkable. At that moment, it hit more than ever before, I was going to be a father. "Let's show this to everyone," I said.

"Yes, let's show our babies off," Bianca replied. We then walked into the kitchen and found the others.

"We have something to show everyone," I said, as I handed the sonogram to Rocco.

"Is this what I think it is?" Rocco said, with a smile. Isabella was standing next to him on his left, while Mason was on his right. Dante was leaning on Mason, trying to get a glimpse as well.

"Whoa, there are two!" Mason pointed out.

"Twins?" Dante said, still not in a position to see for himself.

"Twin boys," Rocco incorrectly stated.

"No, a boy and a girl," Bianca replied.

"Oh, I see now. I made out the boy and spoke too soon," Rocco said, in an attempt to explain his inaccurate observation.

"Isn't it great?" Isabella stated.

"It's amazing. Congratulations!" Rocco said, as he handed the sonogram to Mason and then gave me a hug.

"Congratulations! I am so happy for you two," Isabella said, following Rocco in on the hugs that continued to Bianca. Mason and Dante followed their lead and expressed their happiness for us. After talking about our exciting news for several minutes, we eventually changed the topic of conversation.

"Have you eaten anything sweetie?" I asked Bianca.

"I can always eat something," Bianca replied.

"You're eating for three; I'm sure you can," Dante added.

"Well, I'm starving," Mason said, with everyone else stating that they felt the same way.

"Do you want to order something?" I inquired.

"Yes, but first I want to know what the hell is going on," Bianca said, which made everyone quickly turn and look at me.

"Once we receive all of the information that we need to clarify the situation, I'll be able to provide you with an honest answer that you deserve," I answered, with a straight face, as everyone else smiled and continued staring at us.

"What? Don't give me this shit!" Bianca said, giving me a look of displeasure.

Before I responded, I got directly in front of her and took hold of her hands. "You don't need to worry about all of this right now. At this moment, just concentrate on food for you and our babies. Trust me, please. When we know everything, then I will tell you. I don't want to cause you to be stressed, in case this turns out to be nothing. Okay, pretty lady."

"Alright, I'll agree with you, if you can honestly tell me that we are safe inside this house," Bianca responded.

"Yes, we are," I said, trying to sound as convincing as possible.

"Okay, we will focus on getting us all something to eat, while you guys find out whatever it is that you need to know," Bianca said.

"Alright, we'll be in the game room if we are needed. Why don't you give our parents a call and give them the good news," I replied.

"I will, but you know that they'll want to talk to you," Bianca said.

"I'll give them a call later. Send my love," I replied, as we exited the kitchen, leaving Bianca and Isabella in there alone. The game room was the big room at the end of the hall. It has everything that you would want in there. We all sat down at the round table in the very back of the room. I sat in the chair that was closest to the wall, Rocco was sitting to my right, Dante to my left, and Mason was sitting across from me. I began telling the "Zane story" word for word. Afterwards, Dante and I revealed what we discovered from our visit with Rush. Collectively, we felt positive that we could accomplish the task that had been set before us. Well, it was more like wishful thinking. At that point, we didn't know where the bombings would happen, who was doing it, and we were not a hundred percent sure on the date. We continued discussing everything, until there was an interruption.

"Boss, I have the info that you requested," Nate said, as he walked in the room.

"Nate! Come here. I want to introduce you to some people," I said. He came to the table and handed me three pieces of paper. "Nathan Cane, this is Mason Dunn and Dante Jackson. They are our partners...they run the firm in Jacksonville," I said, while Nate was shaking their hands.

"Nate is a friend of ours," Rocco said to Mason and Dante.

"Thank you for this," I said to Nate, as I held up the papers that he brought in.

"You're welcome," Nate replied.

"We need a few guys sent to Rushon Little's home; he's now a client," I said.

"When did this happen?" Nate asked.

"Recently! We have reason to believe that he may need protection and we are going to provide it. We need you to take care of that, while we are busy with other things. I want the guys you send to report to you. No one should be on his property or come in contact with him without your approval.

Get a short list of people that he will allow to visit and do a background check on each one. He doesn't leave his home, unless he is given permission," I said to Nate.

"I will take care of it. Is there anything else that I can help you with?" Nate asked.

"How is your relationship with your brother Ethan?" I asked. Ethan Cane was an up-and-coming defense attorney, in his early thirties, which Nate never talked about; at least, not to me.

"It's okay, but we're not that close. He has his life and I have mine. We see each other during the holidays, but that's about it," Nate answered.

"Why is that?" I asked.

"He works all the time and when he's not; I'm not in his circle of successful friends that he hangs with," he replied.

"Well, is he good at his job?" I asked.

"According to him he is," Nate answered.

"Does he believe in attorney-client privilege?" Rocco asked.

"Religiously! I know he has good stories, but he won't tell me. Why? Who needs a lawyer?" Nate said.

"Tomorrow, Rush will be seeking new council. Take him to Ethan and let Rush handle the rest," I said. I wanted to find out if I could trust Ethan and let Nate hook his brother up with a high profile client.

"Okay, I can do that," he replied.

"You have been working for us for six months now and we haven't really talked about what you want for the future," I stated.

"I like working for you guys and I enjoy what I am doing right now. I really don't think about the future, I live in the now," Nate responded.

"Are you a cop or involved with any government agency?" Rocco asked.

"No, and it's not in my future plans," Nate answered, with a confused look on his face.

"What if you were an FBI Agent and you had someone detained that was a known member of a terrorist organization. His partner was shot and before he died, he told you that there was a bomb in Miami and it would go off in two hours. What would you do?" I asked.

"Myself, I would use my computer skills and try to find the location of the bomb. If I didn't have any luck in the first thirty minutes, I would beat on him for the next hour and a half," Nate answered.

"Why not start with the beat down?" Mason asked.

"I'm not the size of you guys; he would probably laugh for two hours," Nate responded, which made us all laugh. Nate was about five foot, seven and about one hundred and fifty pounds. All of us were at least four inches taller and about fifty pounds heavier.

"There is something that I think you can help us with. I can't tell you what it is, until you agree to do it…whatever it may be. If you think that you would rather stay away from an unknown assignment; we will completely understand. I like you and you are doing a great job with the business. I hope none of this scares you away," I said to Nate.

"You won't be committing a murder," Mason explained.

"…Robbing a bank or stealing anything," Dante added.

"It's for a good cause," Rocco said.

"I'm in! One of the main reasons that I started working with you guys is that I had a feeling that it would never be boring," Nate stated.

"You won't be disappointed," Mason said, while looking at Nate.

"So, what is it?" Nate asked.

"Everything that is said here, is not to be repeated to anyone outside of this room," I said, while Mason rose up from his chair. He walked over and stood beside Nate.

"There's a code that the guys at this table abide by. Are you sure that you're up for that?" Mason stated.

"I am," Nate replied.

"Then take a seat," Mason said, as he pulled out the chair for Nate and he sat down.

"We are not the mob," I said, in an attempt to clarify things.

"Unfortunately," Rocco quickly added, which brought smiles to everyone in the room.

"Everything that's said here has to stay here," Mason said, now standing with his back against the wall close to me and Rocco.

"Were you not listening? Kastle just said that, two seconds ago!" Rocco said.

"I heard him. I just wanted to stress the importance of being discreet. There are lives at stake," Mason responded.

"Yeah, more than three hundred thousand," Dante added.

"Whoa! What are we talking about here?" Nate asked.

"Three bombings at three different locations," Dante answered.

"A terrorists attack?" Nate asked.

"Yes," I answered.

"We have to contact the police, the F.B.I., Homeland Security…somebody," Nate said.

"Negative!" Mason replied.

"No cops!" Rocco stated.

"All we know is that there is a good chance that it will happen on October the first. We need you to find out more for us," I said.

"If I'm caught hacking into government files to get that information, it'll look like I'm helping the terrorists. Everything that I look for will be red flagged," Nate said.

"The government doesn't know anything about it," Dante explained.

"We can't tell anyone what we know. Everyone we care about will die, if we do," Mason added.

"These people are connected. We can only trust the ones in our circle," Rocco stated.

"Why did they come to you guys with this?" Nate asked, as he glanced at everyone at the table.

"They're pissed! Three of their associates were spread up and down the Atlantic. They want us to pay for it, by knowing about the bombings beforehand and not be able to stop it," Mason said.

"We need your help to do this," I said.

"I'll try, but the combat stuff is not for me. I will help in any way I can; preferably, in front of a computer," Nate said.

"That's what we need from you," I said.

"Let me go and get my laptop, then I'll get started," Nate replied.

"Alright, let's get to it," I said, as Nate got up from his chair and departed from the room.

"Are you sure we can trust this guy?" Dante asked, while Mason returned to his previous spot at the table.

"I've been feeling him out for the past six months; it seems like he's on the level. I had Gus check him out, just to be safe. I trust him and I think he can really help," I said.

"How old is he? He looks young," Dante said.

"Twenty five," I answered, which was only a few years younger than all of us.

"Can't Gus do everything he can?" Mason asked.

"Well, Gus isn't here. Is he?" Rocco stated.

"Yeah, Gus is the best. When he arrives they both can work on it. We need to find these bombs and the targets, as soon as possible. Saturday will be here before we know it. We all will keep an eye on Nate, but I don't believe that there is anything to worry about," I said.

"Gus won't like us bringing in an outsider," Dante responded.

"Nate is a friend. He should be okay with it," I stated.

"Hopefully he will understand that the four of us can't be in three places at once and there won't be a problem," Mason said.

"Oh, there will be a problem; he's old school. No new members, until everyone votes," Dante replied.

"Everyone has! When he did the background check and recovered nothing; his vote was cast," Rocco said.

"He'll be cool. Give him a call and see where he is. We need to be prepared, as if this is going down tomorrow," I said.

"We need firepower," Mason replied, with a smile.

"And a lot of it," Dante added.

"I'll get everything that we'll need," Mason stated.

"You guys go and take care of that. Help Gus get settled in and let him know where we are. I'll stay here with Nate to see what we can come up with," I said, while Nate was entering the room carrying his laptop.

"Okay, we're out," Dante said, as he and the others gave me a fist bump, once they got up from the table.

"Keep us informed on everything that you come up with," Rocco said.

"I will. If you guys come up with any ideas, call me," I replied.

"We'll stay in touch," Mason said, and then exited the room with the others.

"Can I get the internet in here?" Nate asked, after he set his laptop on the table and sat down to the right of me.

"Yeah, there is a wireless connection setup in here," I answered.

"Where do you want to start?" Nate asked, seeming very happy to be involved with his assignment.

"All of the big events that are taking place on October the first," I said, which prompted Nate to begin typing. "I'm thinking sporting events, but explore everything. Check out large airports and train stations. We are looking for three locations that will have a hundred thousand people in attendance."

"I'll start with the largest venues and go from there," Nate responded.

"Start at college football stadiums," I said, after I thought about all of the sports that would be played that day. College football had the only venues that could reach that large number.

"Okay, there are well more than ten possibilities that could fit in this scenario. They are spread from coast to coast," Nate replied, as I moved my chair closer to his to get a view of the screen. We continued working all day and most of the night. We came up with a short list of potential targets, but there was nothing to support our theories. Rocco and the guys did not have any luck either, but they were able to get the weapons we needed.

Gus arrived in Miami and the guys caught him up to speed. Gus took his wife to her sister's house in Key West and stayed there for the night. He planned to hook up with us on the following day, after he received feedback from his contacts. There was little success achieved on Monday, September 27, 2004, but it was a hell of a day.

Chapter 5
The Red Phone

On Tuesday, September 28, 2004, Nate and I had things to do before we continued the frustrating task that we had waiting for us. Gus and the guys were working on it in our absence, while we were out of pocket. Nate and Rush had their meeting with Ethan, while I was helping out a friend. Over the summer, I had been going to a local high school and working with the baseball team. It was more like just hanging out there. I did throw some batting practice a few times; other than that, I told baseball stories and answered a lot of questions. On that day, I was going there to help out a kid that I had grown pretty fond of. There was a scout coming to do a personal tryout with him and he wanted me to pitch to him. I would not have gone, but I figured the guys had everything under control. I knew that they would call, if something came up.

I arrived at the high school at eight o'clock. I did some stretching and running, then began to warm up. After a few throws, a strange man approached me.

"Hi there! I see that your form hasn't changed," the man said.

"Do I know you?" I replied.

"My name is Larry Prescott. I scouted you out of high school; boy did I love you. You know the Marlins were going to draft you, but the Dodgers picked one spot ahead of us. I was truly crushed. If we could have gotten you, your career would have been hall of fame caliber," Larry said.

"You think so?" I asked.

"Without a doubt! The Dodgers wore your arm out in your first season. You should have been brought along slowly. Your first injury came late in the season; didn't it?" Larry responded.

"Yeah, it did. You know... the Dodgers drafted a Joe Prescott two years ago," I said.

"That's my son. He loves football more and I'm glad he does," he replied.

"He's good! Ohio State looks tough this year," I added.

"They have a hell of a team. A National Championship could be in the future," Larry said, causing the both of us to smile.

"We'll see," I responded.

"So, what brings you out here?" Larry asked.

"I'm here to help out Hector. This kid has it all. He's an amazing hitter and he has power. He can steal bases. He has unbelievable range at shortstop and he has a canon for an arm. He's the total package," I said, in an attempt to hype my friend up.

"So, are you going to bring your best stuff or are you going to lob it to him?" He asked, with a slight grin.

"I don't lay down for anybody! Obviously, my arm isn't what it once was, but I'll do the best that I can," I replied.

"Well, I'll let you finish warming up," he said.

"Go take a seat and get ready to be amazed. It was a pleasure to meet you," I replied.

"The pleasure was all mine," Larry stated, as we shook hands before he walked off.

Hector's tryout consisted of batting practice, running the bases, and then fielding. The tryout began with me pitching to Hector. I threw at least twenty balls, using a variety of pitches, locating the ball to different parts of the plate and really showcasing Hector's hitting abilities. Afterwards, I took a seat in the dugout and watched the remainder of the tryout. During the base stealing exhibition, Larry joined me in the dugout.

"The kid is something! No question; a first round pick," Larry said, as he walked up and sat down beside me.

"Do you think so?" I asked.

"I do. You know you looked good out there too," he replied.

"What are you talking about? He hit everything I threw," I responded.

"You did what you set out to do. It was pretty impressive. You were in complete control the entire time. You put the ball where you wanted it; you switched up speeds, and had excellent movement on your breaking pitches. Your fastball is just enough to be effective, for a couple of innings anyway," Larry said.

"I'm glad I didn't totally embarrass myself," I replied.

"I believe you can be pitching for the Marlins within a year from now, if you can deal with coming out of the pen," Larry responded.

"No way, I've moved on," I said.

"Come on, I'm offering you a second chance that I know you've been waiting for. Why else would you be out here? It's still in you," Larry responded.

"I'm flattered that you think I have what it takes, but I really have moved on. I have no interest in playing ball again," I replied.

"I know it takes a lot for ballplayers to move on from the game they love. You were forced to give up on your dream and I know it was hard, but you can do this. I know it," Larry said.

"I'm going have to decline, but thanks for the offer," I said.

"I'm going to let you think about it for a few days. I'll be out of town for a week. Next Tuesday, meet with me and give me your answer," Larry replied.

"Okay, I'll think about it," I replied, as my phone began to ring. I answered it and Larry waved goodbye, as he walked back onto the field.

"Nate! How is everything going?" I said.

"It went great. I'm leaving Rush's now," Nate replied.

"Stop by and see me at Armstead High School. I'm in the dugout at the baseball field," I said.

"Okay, I'm on the way," Nate replied.

"I'll see you when you get here," I said. I continued watching the tryout, while I was waiting for Nate. Hector was doing great; he was now showing his fielding skills. Nate arrived ten minutes later and joined me in the dugout.

"What are you doing here?" Nate curiously asked.

"I'm getting some fresh air; it's going to be a long day," I said, as I watched Hector do his thing. "I like coming out here, it helps me think."

"Have you come up with anything?" Nate asked.

"I've got nothing," I replied.

"Has anyone had any luck?" Nate asked.

"…Not that I know of. Everyone is meeting up at eleven. We'll know more then," I said, looking down at my phone, which showed that it was ten o'clock in the morning. "Did the meeting go smoothly?"

"Yeah, we made my brother happy. I got an invitation to dinner on my way here and that has never happened," Nate said.

"That's great, but I need you to work tonight. In fact, we need to get back home and get started," I replied, after I saw the tryout had ended.

"I've already told him that I had plans and asked for a rain check," Nate replied, while we both were exiting the dugout.

"Awesome," I said, as Hector and Larry met us on our way out.

"Thanks for coming, I really appreciate it," Hector said, as he shook my hand.

"You're welcome. You were really great out there," I replied.

"Think about what I said," Larry said, as I shook his hand.

"I will," I replied, and then walked off with Nate beside me.

"What was that about?" Nate asked, as we were walking toward the parking lot.

"Over the summer I met Hector and started working with him. Today he had a tryout for a Marlin scout and I agreed to pitch to him," I replied.

"That's right, you were a pitcher. I take it, that it went well," Nate said.

"Yeah, well enough for Larry Prescott to offer me a shot with the Marlins," I responded.

"Are you going to do it?" Nate asked.

"No, I'm done with baseball. I came here to help out the kid. I didn't do it to get another opportunity," I said, as we continued walking, now in the parking lot with our vehicles not too far away.

"You never know..., this could be fate. You might want to take some time and think about it," Nate said.

"It's over. I have moved on," I responded, as I began to think about what Nate had said. A thought came to me that caused me to stop cold in my tracks. "Wasn't Ohio State on the list of possible targets?" I said, as we both stood a couple of feet from the back of my Ferrari.

"Yes, their stadium has a capacity over a hundred thousand. What made you think of Ohio State?" Nate said.

"The scout I met over there, has a son that plays for them," I answered.

"Joe Prescott, the quarterback?" Nate asked.

"Yeah. It may not amount to anything, but it's worth checking out," I stated.

"I'll do it," he replied.

"Let's get out of here," I said. We hopped in our cars and Nate followed me to my house. Upon arriving, I opened the garage door and parked inside. Nate parked his Jeep Wrangler beside my black, Cadillac Escalade and walked in the garage carrying his laptop, just as the door was closing behind him. Bianca and I had three cars: the Escalade, which was mine, the Range Rover was hers, and the Ferrari.

"Go ahead and get started, while I jump in the shower. The guys should be over soon," I said, as we were entering the house.

"Would it be okay if my girlfriend stops by to see me, before she goes to work? I had to cancel our date last night and she wasn't too happy," Nate said.

"Yeah, but she can't know anything about what we're working on," I replied.

"I remember the conversation from yesterday. Hell, I can't stop thinking about it. You have my word, she will never know about any of this," Nate said.

"Look, invite her over for dinner tonight. It will give you an opportunity to make up for last night. I need you working on this, until then," I stated.

"She will like that. Thank you. I will be in the back working, until she gets here," Nate said, as he walked toward the game room and I went to find Bianca to see how she was doing.

"Hey beautiful!" I said, as I walked in the kitchen.

"Hey babe! How did the tryout go?" Bianca replied, while I grabbed a Powerade from the fridge.

"It went great! The scout was impressed by Hector and by me. Baby, I could be a Marlin," I said, after taking a couple of swallows of Powerade.

"What are you talking about?" She responded.

"The scout that was there, offered me another shot, but I turned him down," I explained, as I walked over and stood beside her at the sink.

"Are you sure you don't want to think about it?" She asked.

"I'm absolutely positive! It feels good to get an offer, but I don't want it as much as I did. My playing days are over. How are you doing?" I replied, as I put my left arm around her and kissed her. I was humbled by the offer, but my arm was killing me; I couldn't pitch again, if I wanted to.

"We are doing great. I'm good and rested from lying around all morning; I feel wonderful," Bianca answered.

"That's good to hear. Do you need anything? Can I help you in here?" I asked.

"No, I can handle it. There is nothing to do anyway, until Isabella gets back from the market. We're having steaks," Bianca said.

"Perfect! A steak sounds good," I responded.

"They all should be here at any time, go and get in the shower," she said.

"I'll be out in a minute," I replied, as Nate walked in the room.

"Wait a second, I want you to meet my girlfriend," Nate said.

"Where is she? We have work to do," I replied.

"I know! She just pulled up," Nate responded, while walking to the door to me her.

"How is that going?" Bianca asked.

"Not great! There is still quite a bit that we need to uncover. Hopefully, Gus has had better luck," I replied.

"When did Gus get here?" Bianca asked.

"Last night," I said, just before Nate and his girlfriend walked into the kitchen. She was an attractive girl, with dark hair. She had on white low-rider jeans and sexy designer glasses, which really grabbed your attention.

"Don't even think about it," Bianca said, which brought a smile to my face. Up until four months ago, Tuesdays were "secretary night." Before she brought it up, it had not even crossed my mind; but, now I was disappointed.

"Lindsay, this is my boss, Kastle and his wife, Bianca," Nate said.

"It's nice to finally meet you. Nate talks about you all of the time," Lindsay said, while she shook my hand.

"It's a pleasure to meet you. I couldn't ask for anyone better. He practically runs the business for me," I responded.

"Which is great, so he'll have more time here with me," Bianca added.

"It's nice to meet you. I love your home, it's beautiful," Lindsay said, as she greeted Bianca.

"Thank you," Bianca replied.

"I love your car. I saw it earlier in the parking lot at the baseball field," Lindsay said.

"Thank you," I said.

"I told Lindsay that she could change here," Nate said.

"Sure, go down the hall and the bathroom is the first door on the right," Bianca replied, as she pointed in that direction.

"Why was she at the school?" I immediately asked, once the bathroom door closed.

"She is a senior there," Nate answered.

"She's cute!" Bianca stated.

"We have some serious shit going on right now and I thought you were aware of that. I need your help and you can't do it behind bars," I said.

"It's cool! She's eighteen," Nate responded.

"Have you verified that?" I asked.

"I have; and I understand the situation. I don't want her to know about any of it, definitely nothing good would come of that," he said and then paused for a second. "I have already invited her to dinner. Do you want me to cancel?"

"As long as she is of age, everything is cool. As for dinner…I believe we can squeeze in a meal. I am going to take a shower," I said.

"I'll say goodbye and get started," Nate replied.

"That sounds good," I responded. Nate exited the kitchen and walked toward the bathroom. "See you in a few minutes," I said to Bianca, as I headed to our bedroom. After my shower, I went straight to the game room.

"How's it coming?" I said, as I was walking toward the back table where Nate was sitting.

"I think I might have something," Nate responded, as I sat down in the chair closest to the wall. He was sitting on my right, with his laptop in front of him.

"What do you got?" I asked, anxiously waiting to hear what he was about to say.

"Ohio State plays Iowa at three o'clock on Saturday. The attendance at the Ohio Stadium is always a hundred thousand plus," Nate said.

"Yeah, and there is five other games that fit the same criteria. We went over this last night," I replied.

"Last night, we did searches on potential targets. Today, I did a search on Zane Cotto. I didn't find anything on him, but I did find one thing about his brother, Ponce. In 1990, Ponce was signed by the Atlanta Braves and flown to the U.S. He was shipped back, when it was uncovered that he had lied about his age; he was fifteen. Would you like to guess the date?" Nate said.

"October the first," I responded.

"Correct! Three years later, he was scouted by the Florida Marlins, but was not signed. The Marlins' Scout was..." Nate said.

"Larry Prescott!" I replied, while cracking a little smile.

"That's not all! Larry Prescott worked for Atlanta in 1990. He didn't work with the Marlins until their first season in 1993 and...on Saturday, the Marlins play the Braves," Nate said.

"No way! That will be too simple," I replied.

"Maybe, but it is something to consider," he responded.

"What time does the game start?"

"The first pitch is at 1:10 P.M. in Atlanta. However, their unlucky employee will not be there. Mr. Prescott will be attending his son's football game in Columbus, Ohio. I hacked into his credit card accounts and found where he has purchased two tickets for the game. Also, there were plane tickets on there to confirm that he would be in Columbus," Nate explained, with an overwhelming look of satisfaction on his face. It was truly an exhilarating feeling for me. It was like finishing a crossword or, more relevant, cracking a big case.

"Bravo! Now we are getting some where," I declared.

"The only thing is that it doesn't fit. The attendance at the Marlins game will only be around fifty thousand," Nate explained.

"Yeah, but it does make sense. I don't expect Zane to make it easy and give us the exact number of would-be casualties. Really, it's hard for me to believe anything he said. This is good stuff. Good job," I said, just before Bianca entered the room.

"Everyone is here!" Bianca shouted, while standing in the doorway.

"On my way," I responded, as she turned around and walked away. "I am going to see the guys in and then I'll be back. Hopefully, they will have some good news to go with ours," I said to Nate, before leaving the room. I got as far as the kitchen before I was met by Bianca, Isabella, Rocco, Gus, Dante, and Mason.

"Gus, it's great to see you. How are you?" I said with a smile, as I shook his hand and put my arm around my friend with the salt-and-pepper hair.

"What do you think? I could be in Europe right now; but instead, I'm here with you knuckleheads," Gus playfully replied.

"Hello," Rocco said, after he set the two bags of groceries on the counter. "Something is different. You seem confident... You know something, don't you?" Rocco said.

"I do! Gus will have to confirm it, but I think we know the location of two of the targets," I responded.

"Where are they?" Dante asked.

"You guys can talk outside, when you light the grill," Bianca said, interrupting us.

"I'll let Nate tell you; he's the one who found it," I said.

"Wait! Who is Nate?" Gus asked.

"No one told you?" I said, as I looked at Rocco and Dante. I turned toward Gus and continued talking. "Nathan Cane is the one I had you do a background check on."

"As an office employee, not in something of this magnitude," Gus responded.

"Is that jealousy I detect in your voice?" Rocco said to Gus with a grin. Gus immediately gave him a glaring look, but said nothing. He continued to listen to what I had to say.

"We felt under the circumstances that we could use his help. I trust him…and he has accomplished more than any of us so far," I responded.

"He is a computer genius," Rocco added.

"Okay, but keep him on a short leash. As far as we know, Zane Cotto could have planted him here six months ago," Gus said.

"Believe me, I have thought about everything," I replied.

"Look, I'm getting hungry. Do you want me to light the grill?" Bianca asked.

"I'm sorry baby! We'll do it," I answered, as I went to her, put my arms around her, and gave her a kiss on the cheek. In the meantime, Isabella's cell phone was ringing.

"Are you going to answer it?" Rocco asked, referring to the noise coming from her handbag.

"That's not my ring tone," Isabella responded, as she went to her handbag and retrieved a red cell phone from it. "This is not mine!" She said, totally confused.

"Well it's not mine! Let me see it," Rocco said, as Isabella handed it to him. "Hello!" Rocco said, answering the mysterious phone. "It's for you," Rocco said, as he took a few steps toward me and then handed it to me.

"Hello," I said.

"Kastle Raines. How is your Tuesday going?" Zane said. I immediately covered the phone up with my hand. "It's him! We need to record this," I said.

"Okay!" Gus said, while digging in the bag that he brought in. I put the phone back up to my ear and began talking to kill time until Gus was ready.

"I didn't think I would ever hear from you again," I said.

"Put me on speaker! I want everyone to hear me. They should know how much danger they are in," Zane demanded.

"Okay, what do you want?" I said, after I switched the phone to speaker and set it on the counter.

"I'm sure you all know who I am. First of all, don't waste your time and try to trace this call. It is scrambled and cannot be traced. It has been twenty-four hours and I am really disappointed in the level of competition that you have brought to the table so far. I am not being challenged and I am getting bored. Since you are no match for me, I am going to have some fun right up to the grand finale. Each day you will be contacted and given a clue to make this more evenly matched. There will be three bombings in different places. None of you or your families will be harmed, unless someone goes to the cops," Zane explained.

"That won't happen," I assured him.

"Today, you'll get a chance to prove it. First, you will get your clue for today. I am going to give you the location of one of the targets. Pick a direction and I will give you the clue. Which one do you want...north, south, east, or west?" Zane said.

"West!" Rocco answered.

"Bad choice! There will not be a bombing on the West Coast. Don't feel bad. Tomorrow you will get another chance," Zane said.

"Give us another chance now. We might not be able to talk to you tomorrow," I replied.

"Sure you will. I went out of my way to make sure that I can speak with you anytime I want. I know you'll answer, when the red phone rings." Zane continued talking to us, quickly changing the subject. "You have received today's clue. Now, I get to have some fun. Earlier today, there was a 2002 Nissan Maxima parked in your driveway that belongs to a Lindsay Clark. There is a cop car at her home as we speak. Her stepfather is a policeman. If she goes home or speaks to either one of her parents, someone's family member will die."

"She doesn't know anything!" I said.

"I know! The rest of your day should be entertaining, don't you think? I know it will be for me. Miss Clark will not be able to go home or talk to her parents until the grand finale happens. She will be a missing person. Do you understand?" Zane said.

"We understand what this means you cocksucker!" Rocco shouted.

"It's nice to hear that there is some fight in somebody. I might be challenged after all. You will receive your next clue tomorrow, good luck," Zane said, before he hung up.

"Who is Lindsay Clark?" Gus asked.

"She is Nate's girlfriend," Bianca answered.

"He introduced us less than an hour ago. She changed clothes here and then went to work," I explained.

"Where does she work?" Dante asked.

"I don't know! Come with me and we'll find out," I replied.

"I'll go and get him!" Mason said, as he went to the game room to get Nate.

"You have really screwed up! We have enough on our plate and now we have to abduct someone. What were you thinking...bringing outsiders around, with all of this going on?" Gus said.

"Don't talk to him like that," Bianca replied.

"Easy honey, let him speak. Gus, don't upset my pregnant wife," I said.

"Yeah, you could force her into labor," Rocco added.

"The women really shouldn't be in here for this," Gus said.

"We are in here, because that sick maniac placed a phone in my bag," Isabella responded.

"Sweetheart, everything will be okay. We'll take care of it," Rocco said, as he comforted his wife.

"Maybe you should step out for a few minutes," I said to Bianca.

"Fine! We'll be outside. Come and join us, when you're finished," Bianca replied. They left the kitchen and we continued our conversation.

"You guys have broken the rules. No person, outside of our circle, should know anything," Gus said.

"Whoa! It happened and we'll deal with it," Dante replied.

"Dante's right!" Rocco said.

"It should have never happened in the first place!" Gus countered.

"You're right. I messed up," I said to Gus.

"Kastle, I have been next to you for the past seven months. You analyze every decision that you make. There has to be a good reason that you let her in the door. I know I'm not the only one who thinks this. Dante, a little help," Rocco said.

"I think he knows he's right and he's just humoring Gus," Dante stated.

"Nate looks up to us and probably talks about us a lot. Since his girl is eighteen and a senior in high school, I wanted her to see that he is really working for me. So, after Nate gave her the same excuse for canceling their date three days in a row, she wouldn't snoop around or cause any problems. But, that happened anyway," I explained.

"There was no way to know that Zane had more games to play," Dante said.

"Yeah, you did the right thing," Rocco said, raising his voice.

"It's done! Go get this girl," Gus said, while Mason and Nate were walking into the kitchen.

"Gus, can you hack into the phone company and cut off her home phone, work phone, her cell, her dad's, and her mom's. When she's picked up, you can turn them back on," I said.

"I can do it!" Nate stated.

"I have to get my equipment out of the car. Where do you want me to set up at?" Gus replied.

"Set up in my office; I'll show you where it is," I answered.

"I'll help you unload it," Dante added.

"Nate, you can turn the phones off and Gus will turn them back on," I stated, before Gus and Dante headed for the door.

"Alright Nate, let's get to it," Rocco said.

"Whose phone are we cutting off?" Nate asked, while Rocco grabbed the recorder.

"Let's walk. There is something that you need to hear," Rocco said. He played the recording for Nate on the way to the game room.

"This is unbelievable," Nate said with a stunned look on his face, once the tape was finished.

"We need you to go and get her as soon as you are done here," I stated.

"Of course! It won't take me long to do this and then I'm out the door," Nate replied.

"It's a good thing the call was recorded, because if I was Nate, I would not have believed us," Mason stated.

"Mason and Dante will bring you to her. Let Mason drive you back here in her car and Dante will follow. Tell her that Mason is a bodyguard and he gets car sick if he doesn't drive," I said.

"Lindsay may not go for that. She doesn't like anyone driving her car," Nate informed us.

"It doesn't matter who drives, but Mason will be in the car. Bring her back here and we will explain the situation," I said, as I tossed my keys to Dante. "Here, take the Escalade."

"Okay, but what do I tell her when she asks why she has to leave? She can't just walk out; she won't. She has a cell phone bill, car note and insurance that she pays for by herself. She is hot and responsible," Nate replied.

"We won't tell her anything! We go in wearing masks, bag and gag her, and haul ass back here," Mason responded, causing Nate's jaw to hit the floor.

"He's kidding," Rocco said.

"Tell her that you got her a part-time job at *Tress Magazine*, working as a photographer's assistant. It pays five hundred a week, but she must start today," I explained.

"I think she will go for that. She hates waiting tables and always talks about quitting," Nate said.

"That will work! Did you just think of that?" Mason asked.

"He's a problem solver. I wished Gus was here to eat his words," Rocco said.

"You know, I really care for her and all of this will probably end of our relationship," Nate said, as he looked up at me.

81

"Don't get ahead of yourself. She may surprise you," I replied.

"Okay, it's done. Let's get a move on!" Nate said, as they rose up from the table. They had to hurry. Her parents could drive to the restaurant or use a neighbor's phone to call one of Lindsay's coworkers.

"We'll be back soon!" Mason said, as they raced out of the room. Rocco and I followed them out, stopping in the kitchen where we were met by Gus.

"Are you all set up?" Rocco asked.

"No, I was thinking that it would be best if I set up someplace else. It's going to be crowded in here with these kids that I don't know. I need my own space where I can operate without constantly looking over my shoulder. I would feel more comfortable elsewhere," Gus stated.

"Okay, whatever you want. We'll accommodate you the best we can," I responded. Gus has his own way of doing stuff and he is effective, so I did not object.

"We can set you up in my basement. I think you'll find it to be exactly what you have in mind," Rocco replied.

"Okay, that should work," Gus said.

"Come on, I'll give you a hand with everything," Rocco replied.

"Hold up! I have something that you need to look into," I said.

"Oh yeah! What did you find out?" Rocco replied.

"At age 15, Ponce Cotto was scouted by Larry Prescott and the Atlanta Braves. He was signed, but the contract was voided on October 1, 1990, after he lied about his age. Three years later, while working for the Marlins, Larry scouted him again; but, he wasn't signed. On Saturday, the Marlins play the Braves in Atlanta. Larry Prescott will be in Columbus, watching his son play, at the Ohio State game," I explained.

"So he's mad, because his brother didn't get a chance to throw a baseball...and you did," Rocco replied.

"The disappearance of his brothers might have a little something to do with it as well," I replied.

"It's a possibility. I'll see what I can find out," Gus responded.

"Alright work your magic; keep us informed. Rocco, get back as soon as you can; I want you here for the Lindsay situation," I said.

"Okay," Rocco replied.

"Oh, there's one more thing. We need you to get the charges dropped against Rush," I said to Gus.

"He did give us the date. So far, most of our intel has come from him," Rocco stated.

"What can I do? Your Hip Hop Superstar was caught red handed," Gus responded.

"You can pay a judge or strong arm some jury members," Rocco replied.

"You know people! You can get this taken care of," I stated.

"I will see what I can do," Gus replied.

"Wonderful! We all appreciate it," I said.

"If there's nothing else, I'll be settling in next door," Gus said, as he took a few steps toward the door.

"There is one more thing," I responded.

"What would that be?" Gus asked.

"We need to make a withdrawal from the offshore account. We will need cash to maneuver in the coming weeks," I stated.

"That is what it's there for. I'll take care of it. Is there anymore items of business to discuss?" Gus said.

"That's all for now," I replied.

"I'll be back soon," Rocco replied, as he followed Gus out of the house. I went to the back patio to see Bianca and to lend a hand with the grill. I notified her that she had a new assistant on her way over and that we would be fitting the bill, until she could get Lindsay on at the magazine; if that was even possible. We would deal with that later, but either way, Lindsay would be paid very well for her services.

Bianca and Isabella had everything under control, so I returned to the kitchen and focused on the task at hand. Lindsay could not go home or go to school; thus, she would be a missing person. Nate would be questioned and probably followed. The significant other is always the prime suspect and we did not need that. I contemplated every option and came up with, what I believed to be, the best way to handle the situation. I wanted to run my idea by Rocco first, but I did not get the chance.

Chapter 6
Miss Clark

Dante, Mason, Nate, and Lindsay arrived while Rocco was still with Gus. They all walked in and came in my direction. Dante was the first to get to me. He sat on a stool beside me at the island bar.

"How did everything go?" I said to Dante, while the rest of them were walking toward us.

"It went smoothly. She was more than happy to quit her job. Hey, check out where she worked," Dante said, as they all walked up. Lindsay was wearing her black uniform that consisted of black pants and a black shirt that had the name of the restaurant embroidered on it, The Horseshoe Steakhouse.

"I see that Nate caught you and Mason up to speed?" I replied.

"I can't believe that you didn't spot that earlier?" Dante stated.

"I saw her before she changed," I said in my defense. Moments later, Nate and Lindsay walked up to the bar and sat across from me; while, Mason headed straight to the fridge.

"I don't follow. What does that have to do with anything?" Nate said.

"The stadium at Ohio State is known as 'the horseshoe,'" Dante explained.

"That's right, I remember seeing that somewhere," Nate replied.

"What are you guys talking about?" Lindsay asked.

"Your former place of business, but that's not important now. What have you been told so far?" I asked.

"That I will be an assistant at *Tress Magazine* and I start today," she answered with a cute smile.

"What happened to your glasses?" I asked.

"I wear contacts most of the time," she replied.

"Okay, let me tell you about your job. You will be my wife's personal assistant here at home, until her maternity leave is over. I want her to do as little as possible. Your regular pay will be five hundred a week and we will work around your school schedule. This week is very unique; thus, you will receive a thousand dollars," I said, which was received enthusiastically.

"I am so excited about this opportunity. Thank you so much! I am curious, though. Why is this week so important?" She asked.

"I will let my beautiful wife answer all the questions that you may have," I replied.

"Okay," Lindsay replied.

"Will you two go and take over the grill, so Bianca and Isabella can give Lindsay some answers?" I said, looking at Dante and Mason. I wanted Bianca there, when we explained the situation, to stress what was at stake.

"Sure thing; be prepared for the best mouthwatering steak that you have ever had," Dante replied, as he and Mason got off their stools.

"Has anyone called Gus?" I said, looking at Dante and Mason.

"That has already been taken care of," Mason replied, while they were walking out of the kitchen.

"Lindsay, can I get you anything to drink?" I asked.

"Yes, that would be great. I will be more than happy to get it myself, if you would point me in the right direction. This is my workplace after all. I might as well go ahead and get started," Lindsay said.

"Good answer! It's the cabinet left of the fridge," I responded. My first impression of her was that she would be a good worker, but I was unsure of her reaction to our mess. I didn't want it to come to kidnapping, but I was mentally preparing myself for it.

"Can I get you anything?" Lindsay asked Nate, as she hopped off of her stool. There was a few seconds of silence before anything was said.

"I'm sorry sweetie; my mind is on my work," Nate replied, while Bianca and Isabella was coming into the kitchen.

"You've been acting weird since we left the restaurant," Lindsay responded. At this time, the front door opened and Rocco walked in.

"I think I know what's bothering your boyfriend. There's something that you need to hear," I said, as she returned to her stool, which was across from me, and placed her glass of sweet tea on the bar.

"This sounds serious," Lindsay said in a joking manner. Her mood suddenly changed after she looked at all of our faces. Rocco pushed play on the recorder, then reached over Nate's shoulder and placed it in the middle of the bar. We listened to the recording in its entirety.

"Is this for real?" Lindsay said in disbelief.

"I'm afraid it is. I am sorry that you are involved. You have to know that this is killing me. You are in danger because of me," Nate replied.

"Actually, she is not, my family is. I know this is hard to believe, but we need your help or someone will die," Bianca replied.

"Nate trusts you, so I guess I can do the same. Yes, I will do whatever you need me to do. But, I don't see how this will work. If I don't tell my parents that I'm okay, they will look for me," Lindsay said. She was quite calm under the circumstances. I was impressed.

"Let me start by telling you that the job that we spoke of, is legit; that's if you still want it," I said.

"It's all surreal. I will have to give you an answer when this is over," Lindsay replied.

"That's understandable," I said.

"The job is yours, whenever you want it," Bianca added.

"Obviously, your school cannot be notified, but I promise that you will be able to go back," I stated.

"We know people. After all of this, you won't have to go back to school until graduation," Rocco said, which produced a smile on Lindsay's face.

"What's the plan boss?" Nate asked.

"I don't know," Rocco replied.

"I was referring to my other boss," Nate explained.

"We need you to call your closest friend and tell her that you are on the way to Vegas to get married. Let her know that you don't want to worry your parents and make sure you say over and over how in love you are. We will hide your car and we need to destroy your phone. I promise you will be reimbursed for it," I said to Lindsay.

"You can have a new phone every week, when this is over," Rocco added.

"I have a lot of numbers in my phone. Can I take the SIM card out?" Lindsay said.

"Yes, you can save it," I replied.

"Wait! Why do I have to destroy it? Why don't I just turn it off?" Lindsay asked.

"For our peace of mind," I replied.

"They just want to make sure that you don't use your phone," Bianca added.

"Okay. I'll call Amy and then I'll demolish it," Lindsay stated.

You two are not to call anyone or leave this house for any reason. Can you handle that?" I said.

"Yes," they both said, simultaneously.

"Look on the bright side, when this is over, you will know if you are ready for marriage," Rocco stated.

"It will be tough, but we all are here to help both of you through this," Isabella added very compassionately.

"Isabella, we need you to go shopping for our guests. Get them anything that they want," I said.

"Sure, I will be happy to," Isabella replied.

"Spend away honey…spend away," Rocco added.

"Get me a wish list together and I'll go this afternoon," Isabella said.

"Since I'll be married, I need a ring. It needs to be at least a full karat, with a platinum band," Lindsay explained.

"Pick her up a mood ring; it will do," I responded.

"Don't worry. I will definitely make up for the missing diamond," Isabella stated.

"Nate, call your brother and tell him that you are eloping, then get rid of your phone," I said.

"That's a good idea. I'll do it after I turn the phones back on," Nate replied.

"Reserve a hotel room in Vegas with your credit card and start a trail that establishes that you two are indeed on your way there. Order some souvenirs from Vegas and have it sent here. Lindsay can give them to her parents when she goes home. She will need a fake I.D. as well," I said.

"A fake I.D.?" Lindsay asked.

"You have to be twenty-one to get into casinos. You will need an I.D. for your father to find. He should still be investigating even after you return," I said.

"Yeah, I can see my dad doing that," Lindsay said.

"Alright, let's take care of this, so we can eat," I said, while I went to the game room with Nate to watch him work. Rocco phoned Gus to invite him for lunch and then went with Mason and Dante to temporarily hide the cars. For the time being, Nate and Lindsay's cars would be in Rocco's garage, until we came up with a permanent solution.

We finally broke bread and enjoyed everyone's company. We sat at two tables that were outside on the patio next to the pool. The guys were at one table and the ladies were at the other. We needed to talk about our next move and Gus did not approve in discussing anything around the girls.

"Do you have anything yet," Dante asked Gus.

"I can't confirm anything yet, but it looks like the stadiums in Columbus and Atlanta are two of the targets. I'm monitoring all government agencies to see if there is any chatter about large amounts of explosives. I have nothing so far. However, all charges against Rushon Little will be dropped on Friday because of an illegal search," Gus said.

"I knew you would come through," Rocco said.

"We need to see what we can find out for ourselves. I say we go to Pier Five to see if we can uncover anything there and have a little chat with Sam Lewis," I said.

"Good idea. Everything that has happened, so far, has been a clue. Maybe there was something that we missed with Sammy," Mason replied.

"Gus, check out all of the cameras surrounding my property. Today was the first time that Lindsay has ever been here. Either Zane had someone watching the house or he installed a camera somewhere in the vicinity," I said.

"You're right. He must be getting a video feed from somewhere," Gus replied.

"Gus! What is up? You're not on the top of your game," Dante said.

"You do seem preoccupied," Mason added.

"If the load is too heavy for you, there is another pair of hands over there that is more than capable of lending you a hand," Rocco said to Gus, as he nodded in Nate's direction.

"I don't have to come up with everything. In fact, I am happy to see that everyone is pitching in. Nate, any help that you can provide will be greatly appreciated," Gus replied, which made us all look at each other. We all were surprised and suspicious of his response.

We finished our meals and everyone made their way back into the house, except for me and Gus.

"I appreciate you making an effort with Nate. I know you don't agree with him being a part of all this," I said.

"You're going with your gut and making wise decisions, I'm proud of you. I'm proud of all of you boys. This is a tough predicament, but you all are dealing with it admirably," Gus replied.

"Thank you, that means a lot. Look, is there something that you are not telling me? I've watched you all day and it seems like something is off with you," I said. Then, for about five seconds there was silence.

"Yes, there is, but I don't want anyone else to know. When you called me I told you that Rita and I were on our way to Paris for a vacation. Actually, it was a 'farewell' vacation. She has a brain tumor and there is nothing left for the doctors to do. She wants to travel the world, before it gets bad," Gus said.

"Gus, I am so sorry. I wish you would have told me," I replied.

"She wanted to travel and enjoy our time together, and then tell everyone," Gus said.

"I wish I could tell you to go on your trip, but we really need you," I replied.

"I would not leave if you did. After we finish this, we will have our time together. She is staying with family down here, so, she is okay with the trip being postponed under these circumstances," Gus said.

"Nevertheless, I am sorry," I replied.

"It has been a tough year. I lost my best friend and now my wife." Banks' death hit us all hard, but Gus was still hurting. I felt sorry for him. "All of this has turned my world upside down. I haven't been focused on business like I should and the business has suffered," Gus said.

"What do you mean?" I asked.

"Dante and Mason are not accustomed to being in charge. They have needed my help with the transition and I haven't been there," Gus explained.

"I had no idea. I wish someone would have told me," I replied.

"They have too much pride to ask for help. I would not have known, if I didn't see the quarterlies last month, Gus said.

"I can't believe they let this happen," I replied.

"A lot has happened this year. Going to work is just not the same for any of us," Gus said.

"It takes time, but we'll get through it. Look, if there is anything that you need, please let me know," I said.

"I appreciate your concern. The only thing I need is for you guys to stop this maniac, so I can get to my vacation," Gus stated.

"We'll do everything we can," I responded, as we walked into the house and rejoined the others.

On Tuesday afternoon Mason, Dante and I rode with Rocco in his Escalade to Pier Five at the Port of Miami. We asked everyone we saw, if they new the whereabouts of Sam Lewis. Nothing turned up at the Pier, but we did have some luck when we stopped in a bar close by; the Pier 7 Pub. The bartender informed us that Sammy was a regular there and he always stops by when his boat comes in. His boat left on Monday afternoon and was to arrive back Wednesday morning. According to the bartender, the bar is notified when boats come in, so there would be extra staff in place to accommodate the amount of customers during a particular shift.

Sam was set to arrive between eight and nine in the morning. We left a fifty-dollar bill for the bartender and then returned home.

Back at the house, we found Gus and Nate working together in the game room. There was nothing new to report, so we began to plan ahead.

"I've talked to all of my contacts and no one knows anything. We're going to have to roll the dice. The explosives should already be in the vicinity of the locations," Gus said, while I was standing beside Mason. Dante, Rocco, Gus and Nate were sitting at the table.

"If they're not, then they should be on the way at anytime," I added.

"You guys need to be in Ohio and Atlanta," Gus stated.

"It's going to be hard to do, while this whack job has us kidnapping teenagers," Dante stated.

"Yeah, there's no telling what we'll be asked to do tomorrow," Mason replied.

"And the next day," Rocco added.

"Zane gave you a phone for a reason. He wants you to investigate. He wants you to search. We have a private jet; use it," Gus said.

"I think we should sit tight. Let's talk to him tomorrow and see if we can confirm that Atlanta and Ohio are targets. If we can't, then we can fly to wherever," I replied.

"We can't be everywhere at once. We could use more bodies," Rocco said.

"There are three bombs. We need to have three teams," Dante added.

"Does anyone have a name in mind?" I asked.

"I can only think of one person that I would want to have my back," Dante said, as he looked at Mason and Rocco. "Do you remember Mo?"

"Wasn't he a sniper?" Mason replied.

"Yeah, he was. He was a hell of a shot too," Dante said.

"I knew of him, but our paths never crossed. I heard he was a stand up guy," Rocco stated.

"Alright, does he live in Jacksonville?" I asked.

"He lives in South Carolina now," Dante said.

"Do you have his number?" Mason asked.

"No, I haven't talked to him in years," Dante replied.

"Not a problem, my protégé can have that for you in a matter of seconds," Gus stated.

"What is his name?" Nate asked.

"Myron Moss," Dante answered.

"Okay, does anyone have a problem with him joining us?" I asked.

"Gus?" Rocco said.

"It's your decision. You know what's at stake. I would talk to him first and feel him out. If you trust him, then get him down here," Gus stated.

"I will speak to him and see where his head is at," Dante replied.

"Okay, is there anyone else?" I asked.

"I know a few guys that we could use, but I wouldn't feel comfortable bringing them all the way in the operation. Their specialties are bomb deactivation. We can have them search the locations, while you guys are playing that asshole's game. I can communicate with them, unless it is necessary for you guys to meet," Gus said.

"We could use a 'bomb squad'," Dante stated.

"I don't see a problem with it. This is too big for just the four of us," Mason said.

"Make sure they are on a short leash," Rocco added.

"Okay, the 'bomb squad' is in. Have them go to Ohio as soon as possible," I said, referring to the football stadium in Columbus.

"I have that number for you," Nate said, as he wrote it down on a piece of paper and slid across the table to Dante.

"I'll give him a call," Dante said, before he left us.

"Do you want me to find the other numbers?" Nate asked.

"No, I'm not sure about their full names. I have their information in my files on my computer. I'll contact them as soon as I get back to Rocco's house," Gus said, as he vacated the room and returned to his own work center, while the rest of us continued searching for anything to investigate the following day.

Chapter 7
Sammy

On Wednesday, September 29, 2004, I began the morning by visiting Rush and then Ethan Cane. I wanted to give Rush the good news and to introduce myself to Ethan. Also, I wanted to make sure that Nate's cover story was holding up.

I made it to Rush's home at eight o'clock. He met me at the door and welcomed me in.

"Kaz! It's good to see you. This must be important, if you're rolling solo," Rush said, as we sat on his leather couch in his living room.

"I have great news. I was informed that the charges against a well-known Hip Hop Artist will be dropped on Friday," I said, with a smile.

"No fucking way!" Rush shouted in total disbelief.

"The judge will rule that there was an illegal search. Since the only thing that they have on you is possession, the case will be dismissed," I explained.

"I don't know how you did it, but I'm truly thankful," he responded.

"I just wanted to stop by and ease your mind. I hope you can keep this to yourself. You can't tell anyone, not even your lawyer," I said.

"Isn't he your lawyer?" Rush asked.

"It's the first time that I used him. I want to get to know him first, before I confide in him. I don't trust attorney-client privilege. He'll have to sweat it out this time. The information you gave us about Zane Cotto was very helpful," I said.

"I guess so, if my charges are dropped twenty-four hours later," he responded.

"There were some people who believed your story and wanted to show their appreciation," I replied.

"Whoever they are? Tell them thank you," Rush said.

"Now, I need your word that you will not say anything about what we've discussed in the past two days," I replied.

"You got it, I won't tell a soul," Rush assured me.

"Now, stay out of trouble. I have to run, but I'll check in with you tomorrow," I said, as we both got up from the couch and headed toward the door.

"Wait, I almost forgot. Your lawyer is wanting me to pursue a lawsuit against my security company that I employed when this occurred," Rush said, as I stopped and looked at him.

"What did you tell him?" I asked.

"I told him not to bring it up. I have read our contract and I know that a lawsuit was impossible, but I couldn't believe that the guy even brought it up. Look, I just wanted you to know who you're dealing with," Rush said.

"I appreciate it. Can you do me a favor?" I asked.

"Anything!" Rush responded with open arms.

"I want you to ask Ethan, if he has talked to Nate and if he has made it to Vegas yet? I was going to stop by and ask, but I have other things to take care of," I said.

"Sure, I can do that. Is the kid really getting married?" Rush said.

"Yep, he and his girl left yesterday," I replied, as I opened the door.

"I'll see you, Kaz. Thanks again," Rush said, as he gave me a hug. Understandably, he was overjoyed that he was not going to prison.

"You're welcome buddy, take care," I said, as I exited his house. I decided to skip my visit to Ethan Cane's office. I took his lawsuit proposal that he made to Rush was made out of jealousy toward his brother, so I didn't want to give him ammo to take us down. I'm sure he was only giving his client all of his options, without looking at the contract that Rush had with us. I wanted to go over there and let him know where his loyalties should lie, but now was not the time. Therefore, I skipped the unannounced drop in and went straight to Pier 5 to wait for Rocco and the guys.

I arrived at Pier 5 and I was surprised at what I saw. There was a large amount of boats up and down the Piers. I was there for about thirty minutes and had not seen Sam. I explored all of the piers, but waited for the guys before I entered the bar. We walked in the pub and found a crowded room. There was a number of people around the bar, sitting at tables, and standing periodically around the room. We did a walk-thru and came across the face that we were looking for.

"There he is," Mason said, as he tapped me on my elbow and motioned to the corner table in the back of the room. We made our way in that direction, looking at him the entire way. He recognized us immediately, as we were walking toward him.

"I knew I would see 'the boys in blue' again. Ladies, let me talk to these gentleman for a few minutes. Here, get us all another round," Sam said, as he gave one of the women a twenty and they walked away. "Please, sit down."

"Sam, we're not cops," I declared, as we took vacant chairs from other tables and crowded around the small table in the corner.

"You are undercover, probably vice. You know, you guys shouldn't be so obvious. Only a cop would ask the bartender about Sam. My friends call me Sammy," he responded.

"Listen here guy! What can you tell us about the day we met you?" Rocco said.

"You were not very forthcoming in our previous meeting. Tell us everything that you know and we'll leave you alone," I stated.

"Or don't and we'll take you out back and waterboard your ass," Rocco added jokingly, which made us all laugh.

"There's no need for threats. I'll be more than happy to cooperate with you fellas," Sammy responded, while glancing at Rocco.

"So tell us what you know," I said.

"Here's how it works. I call a number and get a meeting place. I bring a black bag filled with cash to the spot and follow the instructions that were given, which are always different. On that day, I caught a cab to the airport, boarded a hotel shuttle bus, and left the bag underneath the last seat. I called the number of the cab company that I was given and I was picked up. The goods were in the back seat along with the coveralls that you like so much. A little while later...I am being pulled out of the cab," Sammy explained.

"Why didn't you tell us this before?" Dante asked.

"I had to see if I was going to be arrested; you gotta keep something in your back pocket to bargain with. Plus, I know who you're after and before, there was no fucking way I was going to say anything," Sammy said.

"And who would that be?" I asked.

"Never show your hand first! Now, that is more like an undercover cop. I know how you guys do it. You get the 'big fish' and make him roll over on the 'whale,'" Sammy said.

"Who are you talking about?" Mason said, while raising his voice.

"Zane Cotto brings all the drugs into Florida for Esteban Ortiz, but I'm sure you guys already know that. Those two guys are untouchable and you won't find anyone who will ever cross them. Don't waste your time," Sammy said, which obviously got our attention.

"Then, why are you running your mouth to us?" Rocco asked.

"Because everything I told you is common knowledge around here. Why do you think all of these boats are in now? Everyone knows that there is a big shipment coming into Miami soon and no one wants to be accused of tipping off the cops if there is a bust. Which is odd, because most all of Cotto's loads are brought to northern Florida or somewhere up the eastern seaboard to avoid the heat in Miami," Sammy stated.

"How do you know that it's his load?" I asked.

"I just do. You don't have to believe me," Sammy said, as he took a sip of his red cocktail.

"Why doesn't he send any loads into Miami?" Rocco asked.

"He brings small loads in that he expects to get busted, just to let the cops save face and keep the heat off his other drop points," Sammy answered.

"You know a lot for a small-time dealer," Dante commented.

"I know a little, but I'm no dealer. I make a little extra money on the side, by giving my coworkers what they need to cope with being out to sea," Sammy replied.

"Well, we enjoyed the chat. Enjoy the rest of your day off," I said, as we stood up and slid our chairs back to the other table.

"I want to thank you guys for not busting me the other day, but this is it. I'm no snitch! I told you everything that I know, so don't expect to get anything else out of me. Unless, you are looking for a rapist or child molester, then I would be glad to hand them to you," Sammy stated.

"Sammy, take care and here, get yourself another round," I said, as I laid a hundred dollar bill on the table.

"Much obliged! You fellas enjoy the rest of your day," Sammy responded, as we walked away. We left the bar and headed to the airport. Mason rode with me in my black Escalade, while Dante and Rocco followed.

We arrived at airport parking, just as Mo's flight was supposed to be arriving. We waited there for him to call and then we would go pick him up. I phoned the guys to come and wait with us, so we could talk.

"What are you guys thinking?" I asked.

"The load that Sammy was talking about is just a distraction for the load of explosives that is coming in elsewhere," Rocco responded.

"We need to find that drop point," Dante stated.

"If it hasn't been dropped already," Mason added.

"I've already called Gus, hopefully he can dig up something," I added.

"Good! I'm tired of sitting on our asses, not being able to do anything," Mason replied.

"Yeah, I'm ready to crack some heads," Dante said, as his phone was ringing.

We went to the front of the airport and picked up Mo. He was about 5'11 and around 180 pounds. He had a well-trimmed mustache, a skinny beard, and cornrows. He was well-dressed and carrying two pieces of Louis Vuitton luggage; he certainly had style. Dante and I got out and greeted him on the sidewalk.

"Mo, it's great to see you bro," Dante said, as he did the shake and hug.

"What's up, Dee? It's been too long," he replied.

"This is Kastle Raines, a close friend of mine," Dante said.

"It's nice to meet you," I said, as I went and shook his hand.

"Nice to meet you," Mo responded.

"Let me get your bags," Dante said, as he proceeded to put his luggage in the back of Rocco's Escalade.

"Nice Cadillac! My boy has really done well for himself," Mo stated.

"It's not mine; I have a Bentley," Dante replied.

"You Florida boys have got it going on," Mo said.

"We're doing alright," Dante responded.

"Now before we go anywhere, I want to know what all of this is about. You didn't tell me too much over the phone," Mo said, which caused Dante and I to move closer to him.

"The man, behind the school bombing in Jacksonville, is going to strike again on Saturday,"

Dante explained while speaking softer than normal, where only the three of us could hear his words.

"How in the hell do you know that?" Mo asked.

"He told us. He blames us for his brother's death and he wants us to pay. He wants us to watch three hundred thousand people die," Dante said.

"Who is he?" Mo asked.

"Zane Cotto! This is all a game to him. Each day he gives us clues to make it interesting," Dante said.

"So, basically he is keeping you guys busy, while something else is going on," Mo replied.

"Exactly!" I responded.

"That's why you're here. We need another person to have our back. I immediately thought of you," Dante replied.

"I'm glad you called!" Mo emphatically stated with a big smile.

"It's good to have you onboard," I stated. Our conversation came to an abrupt halt, when a patrol car, which was rolling up on us, grabbed our attention. We immediately jumped in our vehicles to avoid a confrontation with airport security, since we were parked in a taxi lane. We departed from the airport and headed home.

Moments later, Zane's red cell phone rang. He informed us that our clue would be given to us, in three hours, at the lighthouse in Juno Beach; which was about two hours away. Mason filled in Rocco and Dante, and then we briefly met back at Rocco's house to arm ourselves before going north.

Gus and Nate lent a hand to assure that we were on the road as soon as possible.

We made it to Juno Beach and located the lighthouse. We were thirty minutes early, which gave us time to investigate. We went over the game plan that we worked up on the way there and found a spot for Mo to set up his sniper rifle. Actually it wasn't his, but it was all that we had. So, who knew how accurate he would be, if it came down to it.

With only a few minutes remaining on our timetable, a man walked up to the lighthouse and leaned up against it. The four of us exited the Escalades and cautiously approached the man. We only brought handguns for protection and of course, Mo, who had the target in his sights from afar; giving us a play by play of the subject's every move in our ear pieces.

"How does it feel to have our lives in the hands of a man that we have just met?" Mason asked me, as he walked beside me.

"I'm not too thrilled. I hope that Dante is right about this guy," I replied.

"How did he seem to you?" Mason asked.

"It's hard to say. I was only around him for thirty seconds. He can score a few points, if this goes smoothly," I responded. While we were walking, the red phone rang, just as the time limit had expired.

"We're here," I said, upon answering the phone. We were now only a few feet away from the man who was waiting for us and he looked extremely nervous.

"I'm checking the outer perimeter," Mo informed us, in our ear pieces.

"There should be a man standing next to the lighthouse," Zane said.

"He's here," I replied.

"He has been instructed to go with you, take him back to Miami. I will call back in five minutes and give you the next clue. I have to say, I am disappointed in the level of competition," Zane said, before hanging up.

"I take it, that you're coming with us," I said to the man leaning against the lighthouse.

"That's what I was paid to do," the man said, as he began walking with us back to our vehicles.

"He's coming with us and we're getting another call in five minutes," I said to everyone including Mo.

"Do you know why you're coming with us?" Rocco asked.

"Not really. I was given a thousand dollars to meet four men and ride with them to Miami," the man answered.

"Who gave you the money?" Mason asked.

"It was sent to me," the man answered, as we arrived at our vehicles.

"Put your hands on the truck. I need to pat you down," Dante said.

"You guys follow us; Mason you drive," I said, as we got in our Cadillac Escalades. Mason drove and I sat in the back, while Rocco and Dante followed. Rocco stopped and picked up Mo; then, we were on our way. Precisely on the five minute mark, the phone rang.

"Okay, what's next?" I said.

"Put me on Speaker!" Zane ordered.

"Go ahead," I replied, after doing what he said.

"Mr. Carpenter, you have twenty grand waiting for you if these men never see your son. Today a piece of paper was slipped into his backpack. These men need to know what is on that piece of paper. It contains a location that they desperately need. If these men contact or go anywhere near your son, your money and business deals will be gone. Have a nice trip, I wish I could be there to watch. Mr. Carpenter, good luck. I will call again tomorrow."

"What the hell is going on?" Mr. Carpenter asked.

"He wants us to force the information we need out of you and he is paying you to keep your mouth shut. It is all part of his little game," I explained.

"What's your name or do you want us to call you Mr. Carpenter?" Mason said, as he looked in the rearview mirror.

"He is not going to give us anything that might lead us to what we need," I stated, after a few seconds of silence.

"Give us your I.D.," Mason said.

"I was instructed not to bring any I.D., money, cell phone, or wear any jewelry," Mr. Carpenter replied.

"Okay, we'll call you Woody," Mason said.

"What do you know about the guy on the phone?" I asked.

"I've talked to him before, but never seen him in person," Woody answered.

"Look, you need to tell us everything that you know," I said. Woody did not respond.

"Let's pull over and make him give it to us," Mason said. Afterwards, his cell phone began to ring. "You can tell us what we want to know and lose some money or lose an arm. You choose," Mason said, just before he answered his phone.

"We will not hurt your family. Tell us what we want to know and we'll leave you alone," I stated. While, Woody kept his mouth shut.

"Rocco needs to stop for gas," Mason said, after his phone call ended.

"Okay, let's stop at the next store that you come to. We'll go ahead and fill up too," I said to Mason. We stopped at a Chevron a couple of minutes later. I gave Mason my gas card to pay at the pump. He pumped the gas, while I stayed in the car. I kept Woody company, just in case he was ready to talk.

When the gas was pumped, Mason approached my window on the passenger side. I rolled the window down.

"Do you guys need anything?" Mason asked.

"Yeah, get us all something to drink. Maybe he'll accept a bribe," I said, as I handed Mason a twenty dollar bill. He began walking toward the store, while I turned around and looked at our passenger in the back seat.

"Is there anything that you want to talk about?" I asked, but there was no response, only a silent stare. Seconds later, the driver's side door abruptly opened. Mason quickly jumped in and started the vehicle.

"We need to go," Mason said frantically.

"What's going on?" I asked, as he put the car in drive.

"Your boy has just robbed the store!" Mason shouted, as he quickly drove us away from the gas pump and back on the road.

"No way!" I responded.

"It's true! I was walking toward the store and I saw Mo pointing a gun in the cashier's face," Mason said.

"I'm calling Rocco," I replied, as I put my phone to my ear.

"This dumb cocksucker just knocked off the store!" Rocco said, as soon as he answered the phone. There was a lot of yelling in the background and it was hard to hear him.

"Did he shoot anybody?" I asked.

"No!" Rocco responded.

"Follow us!" I yelled.

"Okay, we will," Rocco replied, before we hung up.

I immediately called Gus to give him the news. "I need you to monitor all police scanners around Juno Beach. The new guy just committed armed robbery at a Chevron somewhere off of Highway 1. I don't think they'll be looking for me, but someone probably got a look at Rocco's plates."

"Where are you now?" Gus asked.

"We are about to be on 95," I answered.

"Banks Newman has just turned over in his grave," Gus stated.

"I know. I'll deal with it. Let us know if anything comes across the wire," I said, as I looked out the window.

"We're screening now. I'll check with my contacts to see if there is anything to worry about and I'll call you back," Gus replied.

"Thank you," I said, prior to hanging up.

"Who are you guys?" Woody asked.

"He speaks! Are you ready to tell us what we need to know?" Mason said, as he turned on to the I-95 South onramp.

"Gus is going to get back to us, when he knows something. Rocco needs to get off the road. Any ideas?" I said to Mason, interrupting their conversation.

"I don't know. All we can do is go as far as we can until he calls. He'll probably have a spot for us," Mason replied.

"I know a place. It's deserted and out of the way," Woody stated.

"Oh, you know a place. That's convenient," I said.

"Sounds like a setup," Mason added.

"I am trying to earn your trust. I think of myself as a smart guy and believe that the best way to stay alive is to help as much as possible," Woody said.

"It helps, but only answers will keep you alive," Mason added.

"There's a place a couple miles up. It's a temporary drop off spot that we use," Woody stated.

"What do you drop off?" Mason asked.

"Drugs! Cocaine, heroine, marijuana, just whatever my associates from the south send," he replied.

"Who are your associates?" I asked.

"I don't know their names. The man on the phone is one," Woody replied.

"Okay Woody, but if we see anyone in the vicinity, we won't hesitate to put a bullet in you," I stated. I didn't want to kill him, but he needed to know that we were not playing around. Plus, I wanted to give him an opportunity to warn us, if there was an ambush waiting for us.

"I guarantee that there will not be a soul there," Woody replied.

"It would be easier to believe you, if you would tell us your name," I said.

"It's Greg," he replied, as I was calling Gus.

"I like Woody better. Where do I need to get off at?" Mason asked.

"Get off at the second exit," he responded.

"Kastle, we haven't heard anything yet. Maybe no one saw what he was driving," Gus stated.

"Alright, keep on it. See if there is a Greg Carpenter from the Juno Beach area," I said, while Greg was giving directions to Mason.

"Okay, give me a second. Stay on the line, while I look," Gus replied. There was silence for about thirty seconds. "There is one: Caucasian, thirty-four years old, 5'7, and 170 pounds. He is single and his place of employment is at a movie store for the past year and a half," Gus informed me.

"What about kids?" I asked.

"No kids…and he has never been married," Gus replied.

"Okay, thanks Gus," I said, before I hung up.

"Where do you work at?" I asked Greg.

"I have worked at J.B. Video for over a year," he answered.

"You must love movies?" Mason stated.

"I do. Plus, a steady job helps keep me off the radar of the police," Woody replied.

"Then, you are probably a fan of his B.F.F.," Mason said, while pointing at me with his right thumb.

"Who would that be?" Woody asked.

"B.F.F.," I said, as I shook my head and smiled.

"Tristan Lake," Mason stated.

"Yeah, I like his movies. Does he really know Tristan Lake?" Woody asked Mason.

"It's true," Mason responded.

"That's hard to believe," Woody said.

"Show him your Call Log," Mason said to me.

"I don't have his name in my phone. I have his alias," I replied.

"What is it?" Mason asked.

"Levi Puckett," I answered.

"I like it," Mason replied.

"Let's get back to what we were talking about," I said.

"Wasn't everything confirmed by your guy?" Woody asked.

"Greg Carpenter doesn't have any kids," I said.

"Yes, I have a son, but he doesn't live with me. If Zane Cotto knows more than you can find on the internet, don't you think that I might be able to answer some questions that you may have," he replied.

"Why do you want to cooperate now?" I asked.

"I needed time to process everything and to decide on my next move," he answered.

"What do you know about Zane Cotto?" I asked.

"A year and a half ago, I was on vocation in Saint Thomas. There, I met a man by the name of Ponce Cotto who changed my life. I was down there, because I had just been fired and wanted to relax before I started a new job. Ponce wanted me to coordinate all drop points from Orlando to Jacksonville. There was a lot of heat in South Florida, so they wanted all of their big shipments to come up north. I set up everything for him and it went smoothly for about a year. After he was killed, everything slowed down. I expected for all of the shipments to stop. I wasn't too happy, but I had made a ton of money and I wasn't in prison. I planned to move, but I got a visit from Zane Cotto. He wanted to speak with me, before our business started back up again. After our meeting, there was far less shipments each month and everything was done strangely after that. Really, I was expecting to get busted at any time, but everything stopped a couple of months ago," he explained.

"You said that you met Zane?" Mason asked.

"Yeah, he showed up with a Latino buddy of his," Woody said.

"Did his buddy have a scar on his face?" I asked.

"Yeah, he did. There was a nasty scar underneath his bottom lip," he answered.

"Did they wear any rings or watches?" Mason asked.

"I don't know. I was nervous. The only thing I remember is that Zane had something around his finger that he rubbed constantly; I guess it was a ring. Take this left," Woody said, as we turned after passing a driving range.

"Okay, go on," I said.

"Zane told me that he had an important shipment coming in a few months and he would give me instructions. A week ago, he informed that the shipment was not drugs and I was not needed. He called last night and told me that I was to go to the lighthouse," he said.

"You are really singing like a canary, but why?" Mason replied, with an excellent question.

"Everything comes to an end. I have made a lot of money and took some huge risks. Now, I would like to live, so I can finally enjoy my life. I thought when the day came and I wasn't needed anymore, I would be killed. I assumed that you guys were sent to do the job. Either way, I am dead. Zane will believe that I told you all everything I know and he will send someone to shut me up," Woody said. Afterwards, my cell began to ring.

"Gus, have you heard any thing?" I asked.

"There is a BOLO out on Rocco's Escalade, but they did not get the plate number. They have not identified Myron yet, but there is a description posted. It has gone out to all law enforcement in a fifty mile radius. You guys need to dump the Escalade fast and deal with your problem," Gus said.

"Thanks, let me know when you know more," I replied, before I hung up. "They are looking for Mo and a white Escalade, but they didn't get Rocco's plates," I informed Mason.

"Well that's good; if they had his plate number, we would have a problem," Mason replied, as we continued traveling southwest.

"What does BOLO mean?" I asked.

"Be on the lookout," Woody stated.

"How do you know that?" Mason asked, as I turned and looked at Woody.

"You can learn a lot by watching movies. In the past year and a half, I've seen every new release that has came out," Woody replied.

"Do you know where we can hide a vehicle?" I asked Woody.

"We are headed to the perfect place," he replied.

"What are we going to do about the convict?" Mason asked.

"It will be up to Dante to decide," I answered.

"He won't be able to do what needs to be done; they've been friends for years. I say we vote," Mason said.

"Woody. What's your vote?" I asked.

"I don't have one," he replied.

"What if we put a gun to your head and forced you to vote?" Mason said.

"I'm pro life. I want everyone to live," Woody replied.

"His vote doesn't count," Mason stated.

"We'll see how it goes, when we get to the hiding place. I want to hear what Dante has to say," I responded.

"Who are you guys?" Woody asked, but there was no response. "Come on, I am helping you out. At lest give me that."

"We're taxpayers that sometimes find themselves in sticky situations," Mason replied.

"Well that was informative," Woody responded.

"You need to find out what your son has in his backpack. We will not hurt him. You have my word," I said to Woody.

"I can believe that, but I haven't met your friends yet," Woody said.

"Where are you taking us?" Mason asked.

"Turn into the old salvage yard, up here on the right. Go to the very back, until you reach a gate. There is a warehouse back in there where you can hide your SUV," Woody said.

"Is this a secure spot?" Mason asked.

"Are there any cameras?" I inquired.

"It's safe and there are no cameras. This is a pickup point for small-time dealers. Since there's no shipment coming in, no one will be coming around," Woody informed us.

"Pull up over there," I said.

"I will open the gate," Woody said.

"Sit tight, Woodrow. I got it," I said, as Mason pulled out of the way. I went and opened the gate for Rocco to go through. Mason followed him in and I closed the gate behind him. I joined Mason and Woody, while they were walking toward the warehouse. Rocco and the others had parked in front of the warehouse door and had already exited the SUV.

"What are we doing?" Rocco asked, as the three of them stood in front of the door. We continued walking toward them.

"This!" Mason said, as his fist landed against Mo's jaw. I pulled back Mason and Dante grabbed Mo, while Rocco stayed out of the way.

"Dante, you better let your boys know what's up," Mo shouted.

"You don't want that. How does your jaw feel?" Mason responded.

"I'll break you in half," Mo replied, as he was being held back by Dante.

"Cut this shit out! We don't have time for this," Dante said, while acting as a peacemaker.

"Oh, I'm sure we can squeeze in a liquor store. I saw one, on the drive in," Rocco replied, which put a grin on most of our faces.

"We have to decide what we're going to do about all of this," Dante stated.

"Does anybody know why the depth of a grave is six feet?" Rocco asked.

"So the rotting corpse is not smelled by animals," Woody answered.

"That's correct," Rocco replied.

"Rocco!" Dante shouted.

"Don't ask, if you don't want to hear the answer," Rocco said with a big smile.

"Come here, let me holler at you," Dante said to Mo.

"What's up, Dee?" Mo said, as they walked away from us.

"You've fucked up!" Dante replied. They kept walking, until they reached a distance that their conversation could not be heard.

"I smell weed," I said.

"Yeah, we burned 'one' on the way. Mo let us have his last joint. It was the least that he could do," Rocco said, as Mason and I shook our heads. "I needed to calm myself. It isn't every day that I'm a wheelman."

"Light it up!" Mason responded.

"Sorry, we tossed the roach before we got here. Now, what are we doing?" Rocco said.

"They're looking for your vehicle and we can't take the chance of them pulling you over with him inside," I replied.

"Why can't he just ride with you," Rocco asked.

"Do you want to take a chance and be on the road when a witness comes forward with your tag number? We can always come back and get it later," I replied.

"Alright! I guess it wouldn't hurt to be on the safe side," Rocco responded.

"Now go and get your soldiers in line," Mason said.

"While you're doing that, we'll be transferring the guns," I stated.

"Let us know, if you need a hand with anything," Mason said.

"I have it under control," Rocco replied, as Mason, Woody, and I walked to the back of Rocco's Escalade and began unloading it. We completed the transfer and hung out by my Escalade. Rocco and Dante pulled the other one in the warehouse. We stood around and waited for several minutes before the three of them appeared. They walked up to us, as we stood beside my SUV. Mo was in the middle of them. He was wearing a cap that he had found in the warehouse. It was white and it had an orange and green U on it.

"I want to apologize for my actions, it was beyond stupid. I am truly sorry," Mo sincerely stated.

"Are you sure about this?' I said, while looking at Dante.

"Is this your final answer?" Mason asked.

"We explained it! He understands what's on the line and he won't cause anymore trouble. Dante will even vouch for him," Rocco said, with a slight grin.

"Mo won't cause any more trouble. You have my word," Dante replied.

"I won't! I know I've made a shitty first impression. I'll do whatever I have to do, to make up for it," Mo said.

"Alright, that's all I needed to hear," Mason stated.

"Okay, let's get on the road," I said, as we piled in and left the salvage yard. We didn't get far, before our focus was turned back on Woody.

"Where does your son live?" Mason asked.

"Does he live in Florida?" I asked.

"No, he doesn't?" Woody replied.

"Does he live in Columbus or Atlanta?" Rocco asked.

"He lives in Atlanta. How did you know that?" Woody replied, with a puzzled look on his face.

"A lucky guess," Rocco replied.

"That's all we needed. We don't have to go near your son," I said.

"And all of your limbs are still in tact," Mason added.

"Where are we dropping him off at?" Dante asked.

"Oh, I'm sorry everybody, this is Woody. He'll be providing us with all of Zane Cotto's drop points for his shipments," I said. Afterwards, everyone introduced themselves and asked their own questions. The conversation continued on the way to Miami, as we caught everyone up to speed and contemplated our next move.

Chapter 8
Old Stomping Ground

On Thursday, September 30, 2004, our day began before sunrise. We boarded our G-IV sometime before 3:00 A.M. It was the four of us, along with Mo and Woody. Mo had a fresh new hair cut, courtesy of Dante, and a clean shave, which slightly changed his appearance. Woody offered to tag along and show us all of the drop points that he knew about. He knew that Zane had a shipment coming in, but he didn't know exactly where. From everything that we had discovered, we felt that the explosives were arriving soon. There were no guarantees that we were right, but it was all that we had to go on. So, we had to give it a shot.

"You have to love flying private," Woody stated, while we were sitting and waiting for takeoff.

"Yeah, it's nice. Show me where we're going on this map," I said, as I handed it to him. I wanted to have a plan all worked out before we landed.

"You don't trust me, do you?" Woody said, as he looked up from the map.

"That's still to be determined," I replied, being completely honest.

"All of my life, I've never had any money. I've always lived pay check to pay check and always in debt. For the past year and a half, I've seen more cash than I could ever dream of having and I haven't spent any of it. I wanted to be smart and not get caught. In the past twenty-four hours, I've been expecting to die at any moment. So, if I was going to die, I wanted to leave something behind that could be traced back to Zane Cotto," Woody said, which was very intriguing.

"What would that be?" I asked.

"These days, investigators are very efficient in their work," he replied, as he took off his left shoe and pulled out the insole. He turned it over and showed me a set of numbers that were on the back.

"A bank account number?" I said.

"It's my account in the British Virgin Islands," he replied, as he set the insole on his lap, then took off his right shoe and revealed another account number on the back of the insole.

"Whose account is that?" I asked.

"After every job, the money I receive comes from this account. I'm pretty sure that it belongs to Zane Cotto," he explained.

"Why are you giving this to me?" I asked.

"If his money was to disappear, it could be used as leverage to stop the events from happening," he answered. I was beginning to be more and more impressed of Woody. I guess you can learn a lot from Motion Picture U.

"He probably has new accounts for this, but I'll see what my guy can come up with," I replied, while I was sending the numbers to Gus via text message. "Why are you doing this?"

"You are my only shot to get out of all of this free and clear. I want to help in any way that I can," he said.

"Good choice. I want you to know that we'll do everything we can to make sure that your family is safe," I said.

"I have no family. My parents died in a car accident twenty years ago. I've never been married and I don't have a son. I just told Zane that I did," he replied.

That's interesting," I said, while I called Gus to have him and Nate work their magic. While we were taking off, Woody reinserted his insoles in his shoes and we got back to the map.

"How do you think all of this will play out?" He asked.

"I don't know," I replied, as I looked down at the map and we finished our plan.

We arrived in Jacksonville a little after 4:00 A.M. Mason and Dante had each of their girlfriends waiting for us with their vehicles. Their lady friends took cabs back home, while we began our operation. Woody and I rode with Mason in his Hummer, while Rocco and Mo were with Dante in his Suburban. We split up and went south on I-95 to the first drop points that we were checking out. Dante started, south of Jacksonville, at St. Augustine Beach. We went, a little south of there, to Summer Haven. Both places were deserted and there were no clues to lead us to believe that anyone had been there recently.

At five o'clock we headed to the next locations. Dante was going to Flagler Beach and we were headed to Ormond Beach, which was about twenty-five miles apart.

"Turn that down," I said to Mason, when my phone began to ring. I looked on the Caller ID and saw that it was Gus.

"Okay," Mason said, as he turned down the volume on the radio.

"We're on our way to Ormond Beach," I said, answering the phone.

"We have a problem! Nate just came across something that you guys need to know," Gus said.

"Is he there with you?" I asked.

"No, he's at your house and I'm at Rocco's," Gus said.

"What's the problem?" I asked.

"A member of your crew has upgraded his status from crook to killer," Gus stated.

"What are you talking about?" I replied.

"Myron Moss is wanted for questioning, by the Myrtle Beach Police, in relation to a murder that occurred Monday night. Kastle, he's a murder suspect. This is not good," Gus stated.

"No it's not!" I emphatically replied. The news surprised me, but with armed robbery already on his rap sheet, I should not have been.

"You know information on a terrorist attack is a great bargaining chip that he'll certainly use," Gus replied.

"I know, we'll handle it," I responded.

"Look, my guys have not found anything in Ohio or Atlanta, so I've instructed them to help you guys in the search. When they get into Florida, I'll get back to you," Gus said.

"Okay, we'll be in touch," I replied.

"Look, they can also take care of the little problem we have. It might be the way to go. You know Dante will not agree with the decision and it will ultimately split the team up," Gus suggested.

"We'll take care of it. If we need assistance, I'll let you know. Talk to you later," I said and then hung up my phone.

"What's up? What did Gus have to say?" Mason asked.

"Mo is a murder suspect," I said to Mason, as I shook my head and he did the same.

"You have got to be kidding me? Dante has screwed up this time," Mason replied.

"It's not his fault, it just happened Monday night," I said.

"And the robbery happened less than twelve hours ago. We have enough on our plate, this bullshit shouldn't be happening," Mason replied.

"He's right!" Woody shouted from the back seat.

"Even Woody thinks he should be popped...majority rules," Mason stated.

"Whoa! Self defense is one thing, but I wish no one to be murdered. Wow...you guys are mobbed up aren't you? I can't believe I didn't recognize this sooner," Woody said.

"Save the mob talk for when Rocco's around. He'll enjoy it. I'm calling Dante," I said, as we continued south on I-95.

"You should call Rocco, if you want the problem solved," Mason said, as I was dialing Dante.

"Kastle, do you have something?" Dante asked.

"You could say that...your boy's a murder suspect in Myrtle Beach," I replied.

"How do you know that?" He asked.

"Gus just called," I answered.

"I'll take care of it. I'll hit you back in a few minutes," Dante said, before we both hung up.

"What did he say?" Mason inquired.

"He's going to chat with him and then call back," I replied.

Dante called about fifteen minutes later. "He's innocent! He can produce an alibi for the whole day."

"Do you believe him or are you just saying that because he's there?" I asked.

"I believe him. Mo called his girlfriend and the manager of his club. The police haven't contacted either of them," Dante replied.

"Alright, I just wanted to get his side of the story. Where are you guys?" I said.

"We're getting off 95 now. We'll call if we have something," Dante explained.

"We're about ten miles behind you, take care," I replied and then hung up. I called Gus and relayed the information that Dante gave me. Gus didn't believe the story, so he was going to investigate a little more and get back to me.

Dante and the guys did not have any luck at the drop point in Flagler Beach. They were back on I-95 South, about twenty miles behind us, when they called. We were now approaching the Ormond Beach exit, which is north of Daytona Beach, on our way to the drop point that Woody told us about. It was about 6:00 A.M. and the morning traffic had yet to begin.

"So, what exactly did you do at these drop points?" Mason asked.

"I was the money man. I would collect the money from the buyers and get it to Zane. I ran the show at the drop point," Woody explained.

"Do you know who he may be using for this shipment?" I inquired.

"I doubt he'll use anybody I know, since he handed me over to you," he replied.

"You never know! He might not be as smart as we think he is or this could be all part of his game," I responded.

"Or…he thought we would've taken you out by now," Mason said.

"Good point. Where do we need to go?" I asked Woody, as we were turned onto the exit ramp.

"We need to take a left on Granada. Go about four miles and then take a right on Beach Street. Then, go about a half of a mile and turn left into a parking lot of an apartment complex. We can see the drop point from there," Woody said, as we were going east on Granada Boulevard. We followed his directions and entered the parking lot.

"Where am I going?" Mason asked.

"Take the parking space in the corner. We'll be able to see the pier from there," Woody replied, while Mason parked his Hummer.

"I don't see anything," I said, as I looked at the pier that was about a hundred yards away; though my view was partially obstructed by a building that was close by the pier.

"Hand me the binoculars," Mason said to Woody, as he pointed to a bag on the back seat. "I won't be long," he said, while stepping out for a better look.

"Where are we going next?" I asked.

"Lighthouse Point," Woody replied, as Mason opened his door and returned to his seat behind the wheel.

"We've got something. There are three vans by the pier, but there's no one around," Mason informed us.

"The usual procedure is to park the vans and then call for a cab. The cab will return after the shipment has been loaded and the boat has gone away," Woody explained.

"That sounds familiar," Mason remarked, as he glanced at me. I immediately called Rocco to tell them the good news and to see how far away they were. It was refreshing to have something to go on, as the pressure was beginning to mound.

"There are three vans at this drop point. We're just waiting for the drivers. Where are you?" I said to Rocco.

"We're casing a bank! Where do you think we're at? We have Rico Snacho in the car. We have to drive the speed limit," Rocco responded.

"Who is Rico Snacho?" I asked.

"He was Italy's most famous bank robber and notorious criminal. The RICO Act was named after him," Rocco replied.

"Yeah," I said in disbelief, along with a subtle laugh.

"It's true, look it up. We're on the way. We should be there in ten minutes," Rocco replied.

"Okay, I'll call back, when we know more," I said and then hung up the phone.

"They're ten minutes away," I stated.

"Are you going to call Gus?" Mason asked.

"I will, when we have more. We need to go check out the vans, first," I replied.

"I'll go," Mason said, as he pulled out a 9mm from underneath his seat. He went to the back of his Hummer and opened the door. He picked up a vest and put it on.

"What kind of vest is that?" Woody asked.

"Dragon skin," I replied, as I took a long look at it. It immediately brought back memories from the last time that I donned one of them and it was definitely a wake-up call for what could easily happen at any moment.

"Look! A cab just pulled up," Woody informed us. There were three men getting out of a cab that was stopped on the side of street. They began to walk on a road that was about fifty yards from the parking lot. Mason opened Woody's door and handed him another bag. He returned to his seat and I phoned Rocco to get their arrival time.

"It's game time! The vans are about to leave," I said.

"We'll be there soon. The exit is a couple of miles up," Rocco replied.

"Okay," I said, before hanging up. Three vans appeared successively, on the road that I spoke of, and thus we began to back out of our parking space. We slowly rolled toward the parking lot exit, while our eyes were fixed on the three vans. The vans turned right and headed north. Aided by the street lights, we could now see that it was three, white, Hawaiian Tropic cargo vans. We pulled out behind them and followed at a safe distance. They turned on Granada Boulevard and were going toward Interstate 95. They were either heading there or continuing on Granada, which turns into Highway 40, and runs into Interstate 75.

"We are on the off ramp," Rocco stated, as soon as I answered the phone.

"They're coming your way. It's three white Hawaiian Tropic Vans. In fact, stay where you're at. Pull over and wait for us there. One or all of them might be going to I-75," I replied.

"Copy that! We're standing by for further instructions," Rocco responded. We continued following the vans underneath the overpass, all three of them were in sequence, going west on Highway 40. Dante's Suburban fell in two cars behind the last van and we were directly behind them. Meanwhile, I called Gus to catch him up to speed.

"We're traveling west on Highway 40, following three, white Hawaiian Tropic vans. We followed them from the drop point."

"Did you see what's inside?" Gus asked.

"No. We arrived too late," I replied.

"I'll have my guys in pursuit as well. I know they're in Florida and on I-75, but I don't have their exact location. Give me the license plate number of the vehicle," Gus stated.

"Call Dante and he'll give it to you. They're in front of us," I responded. We could have pulled up to the vans, but I didn't want to make them suspicious.

"Okay, keep me updated and be careful," Gus replied.

"Will do," I said, as the conversation ended.

"Here you go," Woody said, as he handed me a dragon skin.

"Gus is sending his 'bomb squad' to meet us. They are somewhere on I-75," I said, while I was putting on the vest.

"That should be interesting. The last edition has been a train wreck. I can only imagine what three more will be like," Mason replied.

"I would feel better, if they never saw us. We need to deal with this, before anyone else gets involved," I said.

"I agree," Mason replied. I called Nate, since Gus was on the phone with Dante, to find out what we had ahead of us. I wanted to find the best place to pull the vans over and have a plan of what we would do with the vans afterwards. Nate quickly found a spot that would work. It was clearly our best option.

"There's a place about eight miles up that is out of the way and has little traffic. We'll pass a pond and then a smaller pond that is next to an old repair garage. If we can get the vans off the road; we can hide them until we have our next move…any suggestions?" I said to Mason.

"The drivers are instructed to not stop for any reason. You'll have to run them off the road," Woody explained.

"I'll shoot their tires out, before I wreck us. Yes, we need to speak with them, but our main objective is to stop them from reaching their destination," Mason stated.

"You're right," I responded.

"I have an idea. Grab the red bag in the back," Mason said to Woody.

"Here you go," Woody said, as he handed the bag to me. I unzipped the bag and pulled out a police light.

"We can try it," I said.

"Dante has one too. Give them a call and let's get a plan together," Mason stated. I called Rocco and they agreed to go along with our plan. We decided, if the light didn't work, Rocco and I would take out the tires.

Just before daybreak, Dante pulled in the passing lane and we followed him. He sped up and pulled beside the first van with the blue lights flashing. Mason stayed in the passing lane, halfway between the last two vans. I motioned to the vans to go to the shoulder. The three vans slowed down for a few seconds, but they quickly sped up again. They maintained the same speed, while we were approaching the first pond. I clicked the safety off and began to take aim on the back tire on the last van. In the meantime, Rocco was doing the same to the first one. I had my sights set and my finger on the trigger. Then…boom I heard a loud noise that drew my attention away from the target. I pulled in my gun and saw Dante's Suburban was bumping the first van off the road. The second and third van was skidded behind it, following the same course. They all came to a stop in front of the pond, which was near the repair shop. We pulled beside them, a couple of feet from the shoulder. The drivers of the first two vans exited the vans quickly and so did we. They had no where to go, but into the pond. The third driver stayed in his van. Mason went to his window and kept his gun aimed at him, while the rest of us surrounded the pond.

"Put your hands on the steering wheel!" I heard Mason yell to the guy in the van, as I moved toward the pond.

"You're surrounded!" Dante shouted at the two men in the middle of the pond, while they both made an object visible in their hand.

"They have grenades!" Rocco screamed. Then…boom! Seconds later…boom!

"Wow!" I said in a state of complete shock.

"That's the craziest shit I've ever seen. Who the fuck are we dealing with?" Mo said, after we all witnessed two men stick grenades in their mouth.

"That's loyalty," Rocco stated.

"There's a shit load of explosives in this one," Mason shouted.

"Let's get out of here!" I yelled.

"I'll drive a van," Dante said.

"I will too," Rocco added.

"That was wild!" Dante said, as we hurried toward the vans.

"Kastle, drive my car. I'll drive this!" Mason shouted, as he walked to the third van.

"Where's the other driver at?" I asked.

"He's in the back," Mason replied, while he pointed at his Hummer and I phoned Gus to tell him what we had witnessed.

"Gus, we need another spot to hide the vans. Two of the guys just blew off their own heads with grenades. We're getting back on the road now. Tell us where we need to go," I said, as I got in the driver's seat and Woody was still in the back.

"Wow! What happened to the third driver?" Gus replied.

"We have him," I answered.

"Continue driving west and I'll get back to you shortly," Gus stated.

"Okay," I replied, as we all pulled back on Highway 40 heading westbound. I was first, then it was the three vans, and Mo brought up the rear in Dante's Suburban.

"Holy shit! I can't believe that just happened," Woody stated. The guy was rattled. Clearly, it was his first time to see anyone get killed.

"Calm down! I know you're freaked out, but you have to pull yourself together. We have to do something with these vans," I told him. Moments later, I received a callback. At that point, we had traveled about a mile.

"Turn right, after the next pond you see," Nate said.

"I'm coming up on one now," I replied.

"Turn there and go a half of a mile. There will be a gravel road, leading to a clearing. It's a heavily wooded area and a good place to hide," Nate explained.

"We just need to get off this highway," I said, as I turned to the right and lead us to the destination that Nate found for us.

"It's the best option that we've got. The only other one is ten miles from there," Nate said.

"This will do, thank you. Stay on the scanners and keep us updated. I'll call back, when we decide what's next," I stated.

"Okay, talk to you later," Nate replied, as we hung up.

"How do they know where we are?" Woody asked.

"They're tracking us by our phones and using a satellite to give us directions," I explained.

We arrived at the clearing that Nate spoke of. On the way in, we saw signs that revealed the area belonged to a deer hunting club. It was a perfect place to lay low, considering it was 7:00 A.M. on a Thursday and hunting season had yet to begin.

We all got out of our vehicles; the majority of us meeting at the back of Mason's Hummer. Mason was the first to get there and to get his hands on the passenger that was bottled up inside. He pulled driver #3 out and pushed him to the ground. His arms were behind his back, with plexicuffs securely around his wrist and there was duck tape around his ankles. Dante and Mo was on the passenger side of his Suburban inspecting the damage, while the rest of us gathered around driver #3 to get some answers. Except for Woody; he stood behind us in the background.

"What's going on over there?" I asked Rocco, after hearing shouting coming from Dante and Mo.

"Mo wasn't supposed to hit the van. Dante pulled his arm back just in time," Rocco explained.

"I thought that was your arm out there," I said.

"If it would've been me, he would've joined the other two in the pond," Rocco replied.

"Why was he driving anyway?" I asked.

"That's his boy! You know Dante doesn't believe in three strikes. I don't want to be anywhere near that dude. I'll be riding back with you guys," Rocco replied.

"You're bailing?" I said, as Dante joined us.

"They no longer need me," Rocco responded.

"We have more duck tape if you need it," I said to Dante.

"I'll even help you apply it," Rocco added.

"It's not that serious. With a little body work, it'll be as good as new," Dante responded, as Mo walked over to all of us. I took a couple of steps and kneeled down beside driver #3, who was lying in the grass.

"Why didn't you use your grenade like your friends did?" I asked him.

"I was told to do that, but I want to live. Those two were crazy. I have no loyalties to their boss. This was my first time to work with these people," he responded.

"Where were you going?" Mason asked, as he held a machete that he got from his Hummer.

"We were going to somewhere in Macon, Georgia. I don't know exactly where, I was supposed to follow the two dummies. There were vehicles there waiting for us. We were to load them up and the job was done," driver #3 explained, while he stared at the machete.

"Well, you're a lot of help!" Rocco replied.

"The one that knows the least is always left behind," Dante added.

"He knows something! If we pistol-whip his ass a few times, he'll talk," Mo stated, as he took a few steps closer to him.

"He doesn't know anything! Weren't you listening?" Woody responded.

"Why are you protecting him?" Dante asked, as he turned and looked at Woody.

"I was just making an observation," Woody responded.

I walked over to him and gave him an option. "You were out line. If you can't handle this, then you need to make a decision. You can tag along, until all of this is over, or you can stay here with this guy."

"I want to go along for the ride. I'm sorry for overstepping. I'll shut up now," Woody replied.

"Smart man," Mason added, while Mo kicked the driver in the gut.

"I did hear something about beer trucks and something about Atlanta," driver #3 said, before Mo had a chance to kick him again.

"See! If we applied a little more pressure, there's no telling what else he would tell us," Mo replied, as he smiled.

"I swear, I've told you everything I know," driver #3 stated.

"What can we use to make him talk?" Mo asked.

"We have grenades…and we know he doesn't care for them," Mason replied, as I walked up to Dante.

"Walk with me," I said. We walked to the back of the Suburban.

"What's up?" Dante asked.

"Is he staying or is he going?" I said, referring to Mo.

"He's starting to come around. He got a little excited back there, but he'll be alright," Dante responded.

"We need to be thinking ahead. If he's going to be a problem in the future, it needs to be taken care of now," I stated.

"What do you think?" Dante asked.

"I would like to give him the benefit of the doubt, but I really don't know him. We brought him in and he's helping us out. But, when this is over, will he keep his mouth shut? That's for you to decide," I said.

"So, it's on me?" Dante replied.

"Yep. Look, I want it to work out, but we have to do what's best for us," I said.

"Family comes first. I'm not going to give up him now; he has one last chance. If he fucks up, I'll take him out myself," Dante stated, while my cell phone was ringing.

"Okay," I replied, before I answered the phone. We started walking back toward the others, while I talked to Gus. He called to inform me that his guys were five minutes away. I passed along the little information that we had and made plans for a return trip to Miami. He also filled me in on current events in Miami. The intel that we got, about the drug shipment, was correct. The D.E.A. busted it at five o'clock that morning.

"The 'bomb squad' is five minutes out. We're done here. He and the vans are staying," I stated. The "bomb squad" was confiscating the explosives and the driver. Gus told me that, sometime in the near future, the ATF would receive an anonymous tip that would lead to the discovery of the explosives. I had my doubts, but I let Gus handle it.

"You mean I have to go through all of this again. I don't know anything!" Driver #3 said.

"Tape his mouth!" I said, as Mason grabbed a roll of duck tape from the back of his hummer and tossed it to Mo.

"This is your last chance to give us something," Mo said, as he peeled the duck tape back.

"I wish I had something to tell you," driver #3 said, speaking softly.

"Sound off like you got a pair!" Mo yelled at him.

"Fuck you! I don't know anything!" Driver #3 shouted.

"I bet you heard that," Rocco said, as he turned toward Mo and smiled.

"Bitch, I will blow your fucking brains out!" Mo said to Driver #3, as he gave him a hard kick in the ribs and then administered the tape over his mouth.

We all mounted up and left the scene. Driver #3 was helpless on the ground, not too far from the three vans that were filled to max capacity with explosives. We returned to Jacksonville to catch our flight. The mission was a success. The explosives did not reach their three destinations and there was a chance that this was over, only confirmation from the "red cell phone" remained.

Chapter 9
Maybe, Maybe Not

We were unsure about our situation, so everyone was making the trip back to Miami. Dante and Mason's unhappy girlfriends brought us back to the airport, after a little persuading of course. Upon boarding, the phone rang. Unfortunately, it was not the "red phone."

"Gus! We're getting on the plane as we speak," I said.

"There may be good news when you arrive. The D.E.A. has a location on Zane and they should have him within the hour."

"Where is he?" I asked, while I took my seat on the plane.

"Saint Thomas. Someone from the bust this morning gave him up. When he's in custody, we can hand over everything to the F.B.I. and this will be over," Gus said.

"I don't think that it is. He has given us everything so far. It can't be this easy."

"Probably not, but it is not our problem. They have more manpower than we do. They have smart agents that can get the job done," Gus stated.

"When he's in custody, we'll let it go. Call me when you hear something," I replied.

"I'll, see you when you arrive," Gus said, as our conversation ended.

"The D.E.A. is picking up Zane within the hour," I announced to everyone.

"Is he in Miami?" Rocco asked.

"Saint Thomas," I answered.

"Where is that?" Mo asked.

"In the Virgin Islands," Dante answered.

"That's great, if it's true," Mason stated and everyone completely agreed.

"Are you guys coming back with us?" Rocco asked Mason and Dante.

"Yeah, we want to see this thing out," Dante replied.

"Gus is going to let us know when he hears something," I said, while the jet was in route to the runway. Rocco and I called home to check on things and to give our arrival time.

We touched down in Miami about an hour later. It was a few minutes past twelve o'clock and we had not received any word from Gus. Once I stepped off the plane the phone rang. We all stopped walking and everyone turned toward me. I grabbed my cell and answered it. "Hello!"

"Kastle, I have an update for you," Nate said.

"Tell me something good," I replied.

"Myron Moss was just arrested. It turns out the Myron Moss that was wanted for murder was from Charleston. They were about the same age and they look alike. Your boy will not be going to jail, at least not for murder," Nate stated.

"Are you sure?" I asked.

"I'm positive," Nate answered.

"Is there any more news?" I asked.

"Not yet," Nate replied, as the "red phone" began to ring.

"Keep me in touch," I said.

"Will do," Nate replied. I hung up and immediately answered the other call.

"Now this is more like it!" Zane stated.

"What's the clue for today?" I asked.

"First, let me congratulate you on your success. This is now a game," Zane said.

"I have to say that you have employees that know the meaning of loyalty," I stated.

"What do you mean?" Zane asked.

"Mr. Carpenter committed suicide before he would tell us anything about you," I stated.

"I knew he wouldn't do anything that may hurt his child. A family man is so predictable. If it wasn't him, then how did you know?" Zane said.

"If we meet face to face, I'll tell you," I responded.

"No, I'm afraid you will be too busy to meet with me. I expected you to have some success, so I didn't tell you the whole truth. There are other targets and the number of causalities is a lot lower," he stated.

"So, how many targets are there?" I asked.

"Wait, there's time. Don't be in such a hurry. You will receive the next clue tomorrow.

Enjoy the rest of your day. Relax and smell some roses," Zane calmly said, before he ended the call.

I passed along a summary of the two calls and we all went back to Rocco's house. Gus verified that Zane evaded the authorities and his whereabouts were unknown. We were back at square one. The only thing we had to go on was the third target that we did not uncover. It could still be in play. Basically, we had nothing and it was frustrating.

We sat on our asses and went over every scenario that we could think of. While we were deep in thought, the news was on. The morning drug bust was a big story, but there was another headline that dominated the broadcast and provided us with something to look into. There was a presidential debate that was being held, later that night, at the University of Pittsburg. Nate did some digging and discovered that President Russell would be going back to D.C. for the weekend. Governor Cruz would be stopping in Philadelphia on Friday, then going to New York on Saturday. He was set to be in Central Park on Saturday and at NYU on Sunday. These events had been scheduled for months, so there was a possibility that Governor Cruz could be part of the plan. President Russell and Governor Cruz were projected to be in a dead heat, with a little more than a month away from Election Day. An assassination plot was definitely something that we had to consider, but truthfully, we were grasping at straws. Zane's target could now be a number of things. We continued researching our theory, since there was nothing productive for us to do, until the "red phone" rang.

After racking our brains for three hours, we decided to get some fresh air and go pay a visit to our favorite police informant. We arrived at his usual hangout, not too far from where the shipment was busted. We could see that the road was blocked off and there were a number of law enforcement personnel in the area. We went inside and found him sitting at his table. Dante and Mo went and sat at the bar, while Mason, Rocco, Woody and I sat down with Sammy.

"Well look who it is, the Po Po. Shouldn't ya'll be patrolling Pier 22?" Sammy said.

"It has been a long day and we wanted to have a drink with a good friend of ours," I replied.

"I can arrange that, as long you guys are buying. Hey ma! Will you get us a round of drinks over here and be sure to get one for yourself," he said to a woman sitting at the table next to ours. "So he must be the rookie?" Sammy said, referring to Woody.

"He is," Mason answered.

"What do you guys want?" Sammy asked.

"We just came for some friendly conversation," I replied.

"Sure you did," Sammy responded, as the woman arrived with our drinks.

"What did you bring us?" Sammy asked.

"Your favorite," she answered.

"That'll work! Thank you honey," Sammy said, as he gave her a wink and took a sip of his drink. "This is the shit."

"It's good. What is it?" Woody asked.

"It's called a Rum Punch," Sammy replied.

"What can you tell us?" Rocco asked.

"I heard that there is a hot tranny running around, disappointing a lot of suckers," Sammy responded.

"You sound like you have had a bad experience recently?" Mason said, as laughter immediately followed.

"Not me, I'm too smart for that to ever happen. I really don't have anything for you boys. I thought you would look down the pier and see that I've given you guys more than enough," Sammy replied.

"We appreciate the info. We just thought there was a chance that you would come through once again," Rocco stated.

"I know nothing," Sammy said, as he turned up his glass.

"You have to know about something?" I responded.

"If you stick around, there's usually a dice game and Three-card Monte in the back room," Sammy stated.

"Come on," Rocco said.

"I would love to help you guys, but everyone is not saying a word about anything. They are scared shitless! Word is, that the shipment was much larger than it was suppose to be and there are some unhappy people," Sammy said.

"Esteban Ortiz?" I asked.

"Yes sir! I hear that they are no longer partners," Sammy replied.

"Well that's something. What else do you know?" Mason asked.

"I don't consider that to be something, I bring stuff much juicier than that to the table," Sammy responded. We continued having small talk for a while, but nothing that we believed would help us was ever produced. We paid for the tab and we left Sammy a hundred dollars.

We returned to Rocco's house and filled in Gus and Nate on the information that Sammy gave us, which was not much help with our current problem. We all brainstormed for most of the night. Although Rocco, Nate, and I took an hour off and went to my house to check on our significant others. Other than that hour, a group of us were steady going over different target possibilities. If we were not staring at a computer screen, then we were discussing any idea that popped in our heads.

When the morning came I left the guys and walked over to my house to take a shower and to get a change of clothes. Bianca was still sleeping, so I wanted to surprise her and make her breakfast. During all of this, there was little time for me to do nice things for her. Rocco was doing the same at his house, while the guys were in his basement taking naps. Nate was the only one working when I left. He was determined to find a lead for us. Gus departed before sunrise to go and eat breakfast with his wife, which was his routine every morning.

After getting cleaned up, I started making breakfast. While I was beginning to start on the omelets, our houseguest joined me in the kitchen.

"How can I help?" Lindsay asked.

"I have it under control for now, take a seat. What can I get you to drink?" I said, as she sat down at the bar.

"Tomato Juice," she replied.

"So, how are you holding up?" I asked, while I placed a glass of tomato juice in front of her.

"I'm hanging in there," she replied, after taking a sip of juice.

"Hopefully you won't have to be here for much longer," I stated.

"I enjoy it here. I hate that it's under these circumstances, but it has been like a mini vacation for me," she said.

"Thank you for making the best out of this. You could have handled it totally different, but you didn't. Nate is a lucky guy to have found someone who's mature, beautiful, and is calm during times of adversity. I'm impressed by the both of you," I stated, as she began to blush.

"Thank you," she said, before looking away. "Did Bianca take all of those pictures?" Lindsay asked, while pointing to the living room.

"Yes she did. Aren't they spectacular?" I stated.

"She is talented. I just love that one." It was a photo of two people on a beach, holding hands and looking at a breathtaking sunset. The photo was taken from behind the couple. The subjects, featured, made "the piece" unique and original.

"That one is my favorite too," I replied.

"I would love to have one."

"I'm sorry, but that's impossible. There's only one other one in the world. The people in the picture will not make another copy."

"Not even for someone who's been kidnapped?" Lindsay said with a grin on her face.

"I'm sorry, I can't. If you have any other requests, I will be happy to grant them."

"Who are the people in the picture?"

"Tristan Lake and Sophie Brees," I said.

"No way!" She said in disbelief.

"It's true. Ask Nate, if you don't believe me," I replied, just before the door bell rang and there were three knocks on the door. "Will you start the omelets, while I get the door?"

"Sure! I make the best omelets," Lindsay responded.

"Okay, we'll see," I said, as I passed her on my way to the front door. I looked out of the window first, to identify the person. I was shocked and unsettled by who I saw on the other side of the door. I quickly went over to the couch and grabbed my gun from underneath the cushion. I kept it down by my side, as I walked to the door and opened it.

"What are you doing here?" I said, as I stood in the doorway.

"Whoa! There's no need for a gat!" Sammy stated, as he was eyeing my gun that was in my right hand and down by my side.

"How did you find me?" I asked.

"I know this is crazy, but my story's even crazier. I was given directions and a thousand dollars to come here and talk to you," Sammy explained.

"Come on, let's go to the garage. I'll meet you over there," I said, as I shut the door and walked through the house to the garage. I opened the garage door and Sammy walked in.

"Your crib is sick and so is this. I bet you can do some real joy riding in that," he said, as he pointed at the Ferrari. "I never thought about being a cop, but if I could live like this; I could stand being called a pig every minute of every day. Seriously, you've got to put me on the payroll. I'll do anything. Do you have a dog? I'll walk behind it, all day, with doggie wipes," Sammy said, as I smiled.

"Why are you here?"

"I'm going to tell you the whole story, but why are we talking out here. I have some great information for you. It should be told over a nice meal that is served to us by a gorgeous woman. Oh, I bet you have a hot trophy wife, don't you?"

"Get to it!"

"After we talked yesterday, I stayed at the pub for about an hour. Then, I went to get a massage. I like to get one whenever I have some extra cash."

"Basically, whenever we come around," I added.

"Yeah, I've been there a lot this week. I was there at the place, laying face down on the table, getting rubbed down. I was thoroughly enjoying myself, until the chic left the room to get more oil. That's when a man told me not to move and don't turn around. He said that he wouldn't hurt me and he only wanted to talk. He told me that he would give me a thousand dollars, if I would come to this address and tell Kastle Raines everything that he said. I had no idea who was going to open the door, but it made sense when I saw you. He said that there were two cargo vans that picked up a shipment from Lighthouse Point yesterday morning. Both vans were loaded with fireworks. One went east and one went north on I-95. He said the cargo was going to bridges in St. Petersburg and Brooklyn. I guess someone is planning a fireworks show."

"Did he say anything else?"

"Yeah, he said to tell you this and only you."

"Did you see his face?"

"No, I didn't move. I did see his fingers when he put the money in my hand. I could tell that he has a tan and he definitely gets manicures."

"Did he have an accent?"

"I don't think so, but I'm not positive. I had a lot going through my mind. The barrel of his pistol was pressed against the back of my head."

"I'm sorry that you had to go through that. We'll take it from here and, of course; you'll be well compensated for your troubles, as long as no one else receives this information."

"Believe me, I want to live. I only have to be warned once."

"That's good to know," I replied, as we began to walk out of the garage.

"Okay, good luck and don't forget about the compensation that you spoke of earlier. I need all the extra cash I can get, to deal with all of the stress I've been experiencing lately," Sammy said.

"Alright, take care," I replied, as I shook his hand and he gradually walked off. I watched him get into a green, Crown Victoria and drive away from the premises. I made a few calls before I went back inside.

"Round up everybody and come to my house. I have what we need," I said, once Rocco picked up the phone.

"I'll be finished with breakfast in a few minutes," Rocco replied.

"We need to be quick; it's going to be a busy day. Look, send Nate over, so he can eat breakfast with his girlfriend."

"Okay, I will."

"See you when you get here," I replied, as our call ended. I went back in the garage and closed the door, before I returned to preparing breakfast. I made a stop by my bedroom to see if my lovely wife would like her breakfast in bed. I normally would not let myself get my hopes up, but for some reason I had a good feeling that this intel was correct. Only time would tell.

Chapter 10
Brooklyn Dodgers

Friday, October 1, had a great beginning. We all had a well deserved breakfast and there was hope that our lives were going to be normal once again. I told everyone exactly what Sammy said. We were skeptical about the reliability of the source, but time was running out. We had to take a chance.

We began to organize a game plan. We needed to split up and go to the different locations. Gus volunteered the "bomb squad" to go to New York, while we went to St. Petersburg. It made the most sense, but I did not trust anyone outside of our group. I felt some of us needed to be there to get the job done, but a part of me just wanted to meet the "bomb squad."

Gus and Nate provided us with a layout of the locations: the Sunshine Skyway Bridge that crosses Tampa Bay and the Brooklyn Bridge. From earlier research, there was a pretty good chance that we knew what the target was in Brooklyn. Nate dug further and discovered that Governor Cruz was scheduled to have a private dinner with his daughter, a freshman at Brooklyn College, at an undetermined location. Then, he was to arrive in Manhattan at 10:00 P.M. His wife was not with him on the trip. She was home with their five-year-old son, who was having his tonsils removed on Monday. Nate's skills were getting better and better; we all were impressed.

We decided that Dante, Mo, and Rocco were going to St. Petersburg. Mason, Woody, and I were going to Brooklyn. I wanted Rocco there to keep an eye on Mo and to make sure the mission would get done. We had Nate work with them and Gus was with us. They had their mission and we had ours.

After doing research, we learned that both Tampa Bay and the East River were heavily monitored since 9/11. Therefore, a strike by sea was unlikely, but it was not totally out of the question. We concluded that the river would only be used as an exit strategy. They would probably place the explosives at night. If they were stealth, it could happen without being detected, but the chances were slim. We covered every angle, on each subject, sometimes contradicting ourselves in doing so.

We worked out our game plan in a swift manner and made arrangements for transportation. Rocco and the guys were going by helicopter, while Mason and I were taking the company jet. We grabbed our gear, spending money, and packed the vehicles before we said our goodbyes. Bianca walked me out, before we departed for the airport.

"Take care of yourself and hurry back to us," Bianca said, as she put her hand on her belly.

"I will and then when I get back, you and our babies will have my full attention forever," I said, once I took hold of her hands and pulled her towards me.

"Just make it back in one piece," she responded.

"I love you," I said, as I leaned in and kissed her lips.

"I love you too," Bianca replied, as we parted ways. I walked to the car and then we got the call.

"Boy, do I have a treat for you!" Zane said, as soon as I answered the "red phone."

"I bet you do," I replied, as the guys crowded around me.

"I have to make up for yesterday. I didn't have any fun. I wanted to be fair and give you enough time to beat the deadline that you have today," Zane said.

"Let's hear it," I replied.

"I can tell by the sound of your voice that this is going to be fun. You'll have to get every item that I want and transport them to a place of my choosing by twelve o'clock tonight. If this is done, I will grant you three wishes twenty-four hours from now," Zane said.

"You were right. This will be fun," I responded.

"I'll send you a list and the destination. Happy hunting," Zane said. He hung up and I received a text a couple of minutes later. It contained a list of ten animals. They were to be delivered to the middle of the Sunshine Skyway Bridge in St. Petersburg at midnight.

"We're going to have to break in a zoo to find these animals," Dante stated. There was a porcupine, chameleon, chimpanzee, and other exotic animals on the list.

"We'll have an expert with us. I'm sure it won't be a problem," Rocco replied. We knew what Zane was up to. None of us wanted to bring animals to a bridge to be killed by a wreck or an explosion. We decided to get to our destinations and then choose our best course of action. I got Nate to beef up security around my house, just in case. Then, we were off to the airport.

We flew to New York and Rocco and the guys went to St. Petersburg by helicopter. Actually they landed in a field, 10 miles south of the Sunshine Skyway Bridge, next to a Salvage yard on Bayshore Drive. Nate discovered that the owner was selling his business because of money problems. The guys informed the man that they were coming there to look at the place. After they arrived, they gave him money to let them use his place for a day or so. His money problems were now solved and he swore to secrecy. He provided them with everything they needed or he pointed them in the right direction. There was a used van in the area that the man went and purchased for them to get around in.

On the way to the salvage yard, they flew over the bridge and saw that the Port of Tampa Bay was monitored heavily. They had to find out how the bombs were going to be placed on the bridge, as did we with our own task in Brooklyn.

At 1:07 P.M., Mason, Woody, and I arrived at LaGuardia Airport in Queens, New York. Gus had the "Bomb Squad" have a vehicle there waiting for us upon our arrival. Gus gave us all of the instructions; the "Bomb Squad" was nowhere to be seen. He passed along the whereabouts of the vehicle and waited for us to call him back when we were on our way. Mason went to get our new wheels and we stayed at the plane with our gear. While we were waiting, I received another call.

"Nate, what's up?"

"There's a guy here that says that he has a package for you and he will only give it to you."

"What's his name?"

"Sammy. He says that he's a friend."

"Let me talk to him."

"Kastle, I went home and there was a package waiting for me. There was ten thousand dollars in it and instructions to get the envelope to you as soon as possible," Sammy stated.

"What's in the envelope?" I asked.

"I haven't looked."

"Hand it to the guy at the door and hang out outside. Don't go anywhere! The guy there has something for you. Remember, no one can ever know what you've given me. You can't tell a soul about any of this," I said.

"Whatever you say. My lips are sealed!" Sammy replied, before he got off the phone.

"There's a letter here that says that the explosives in the vans were created by Zane Cotto.

It's a large number of mini-bombs that are controlled by a single computer. It states that there is a video on a disk that shows how it works," Nate said. He put it in and explained the contents of the video to me. There was a small object, about the size of a pebble, placed in the tread of a tire that was on a small car. It showed some sort of computer inside a metal case that detonates the bomb. The car blows up. Only one of the small devices was used. There was dialogue that stated that the computer could set off any of the devices in a ten mile radius. It was explained that the device was armed by pushing a single button on the computer. This would cause the device to go to the nearest piece of metal, like a magnet. There was a two minute timer on the computer that was started once the devices were activated. When the time elapsed, a signal would go to the devices, which would make the mini-bombs explode and ignite anything flammable within ten feet of it, like the fuel tank; the more devices in the proximity, the bigger and the more powerful the explosion.

Nate sent the video to Gus. I instructed him to go into my safe and get ten thousand dollars to give to Sammy. I had to take care of him like I promised and I was hoping that he would not talk. I liked him. I let Nate go, so he could pass along the new information to the others and give Sammy his money. I called Gus and we pondered our next move.

A part of me wanted to be involved in both of the plans, but I stayed out of the way. Rocco and Dante knew what they were doing, so I focused strictly on New York. It was the main priority, because it made the most sense. The Brooklyn Bridge would be well populated and a high profile political figure would be one of them. It would be a perfect place to unveil a new bomb that was going to be sold to the highest bidder.

Gus informed me that the "bomb squad" was trying to locate the white cargo van. While, he was in the process of getting more information about the bomb that was on the video. He told me that, on the video, the computer was inside a room. Therefore, we determined that a satellite was needed for everything to work and we should have that in mind, while we were searching for the white van. We were basically lost at this point. The only thing that we had to go on was the time that the bombings would happen. We were guessing that the mini car-bombs would be set off once the Governor crossed the Brooklyn Bridge. We did not know if we could trust the information that was sent to us, since it came from an unknown source. For all we knew, it could have been Zane Cotto evening the odds in our little game. Primarily, we needed to find the van before the mini-bombs were dropped on the bridge or find the computer. Gus was tracking the Governor, so we knew where he was at all times. I got off the phone with Gus to let him do his thing.

We loaded the Blue, GMC Yukon and Mason just drove us around. We were trying to find the van, but we felt the chances of that actually happening were slim to none. Mason, Woody, and I put our heads together and attempted to come up with something that would help us. Around that time is when we heard a cell phone ringing that was coming from the glove compartment. I opened it up and saw a black cell phone. I took it out and shut the compartment door.

"That's Samsung's latest and greatest," Mason stated.

"Oh, that's the new 'Ice Phone.' It's not supposed to come out until December," Woody added.

"I have one back in Jacksonville," Mason said.

"Bianca has one," I said.

"I know a guy. I can hook you up with one," Mason said, as he turned and looked at Woody.

"It says unknown. I'm going to answer it. Hello," I said, as I set it to speaker for everyone to hear.

"I thought we should talk," a voice said. The person on the line was disguising his voice using an electronic voice distorter.

"Who am I talking to?" I asked.

"That's not important. We're working together and that's all you need to know. We'll never see each other and you'll never hear my voice. If we must have names, you can call me Oscar and I'll call you Romeo. Are you okay with that?" He said.

"Whatever! I want to get this done as soon as possible," I responded.

"I called to let you know where we are. We have a man following the Governor's every move and we're twenty minutes away from the helicopter. Your team will be on the ground waiting for further instructions, while we're scanning the area from above," Oscar said.

"Okay, that sounds good. Good luck," I replied.

"We don't need luck. We're good at our job. Be ready and try to answer the phone before it rings four times. There might be something important that you amateurs might need to know," Oscar said, as he cut us off before anyone could respond.

"What an asshole!" Woody said from the back seat.

"He's a prick! I don't like this shit at all! We don't know who they are or if we can trust them. They could have their own agenda and we may be a part of something that we don't agree with," Mason stated.

"A conspiracy... I don't know. We need to do what we came here to do, even if we have to do it ourselves. If Oscar and the 'Bomb Squad' can help us, so be it," I replied.

"I'm just saying that we need to be thinking about every scenario before each move we make. Come on, this guy was making jokes when we're nowhere," Mason said.

"He doesn't sound too professional, does he?" Woody added.

"I would like to stick that 'Ice Phone' up his professional ass," Mason stated.

"Let me see the phone. Is it true that the text alert sounds like flowing water?" Woody said.

"It's more like a waterfall," Mason responded, as I stared back at Woody.

"I'm nervous back here. I need a distraction," Woody replied.

"Have a ball," I said, as I tossed the 'Ice Phone' to him. He browsed through the features and we got busy with our search.

We humored Oscar and checked out everything that was asked of us. We went to Queens, Brooklyn, and Manhattan. At around 5:00 P.M., after having no luck whatsoever, we received a break by the way of another phone call.

"This should be interesting," Mason said, as he looked at me after the "red phone" started to ring.

"Hello!" I said, after I turned on the speakerphone.

"I have some new information for you," a voice said, that was disguised by the popular voice distorter.

"We know who you are. Why are you disguising your voice?" I stated.

"This is not Zane Cotto. I'm the one who sent a messenger to you. Did you receive the video?" He said.

"We did! Thank you," I replied.

"I have one of Zane's men here and he gave me this number. He also told me the whole plan and I wanted you to get the correct information. The van going to St. Petersburg is loaded with a computer that is in a silver, metal case that controls the 'mini bombs.' There's only a two mile radius with this one because there is no satellite for it. A van will drop the bombs on the Skyway Bridge, while in the north bound lane. The computer will be in a van going south. It's supposed to happen at midnight," he said.

"What about the other one?" I asked eagerly.

"The computer that was on the video is in New York and it is in a silver metal case. It is set up on the top of a parking garage somewhere near the Brooklyn Bridge. According to his man here, you can see the bridge from there. The main target is the cars on the bridge, but there will be a lot of traffic in a ten mile radius with the hundreds of mini-bombs everywhere. It is set to take place when Governor Cruz is on the bridge," he stated.

"Why is he targeting bridges?" Mason asked.

"Zane wants people to have fear when they are on a bridge," he replied.

"I would love to thank you in person, when this is over," I said.

"We'll see how this plays out. Good luck," he said, before hanging up.

"Whoever that was, doesn't want this to happen," I said.

"No he doesn't," Mason added.

"I don't know what's going on. I'm totally blown away with all of the strange voices, the secrecy, and the inside info. I'm beyond confused," Woody stated.

"Isn't it fun? Aren't you glad you tagged along?" Mason responded, looking back at Woody.

"Yes I am. This is going to be something that I'll never forget. It sucks though, because I can never tell anybody about what I've seen. But, that's okay; I'll just enjoy the ride," Woody said.

"That's the right attitude," Mason replied.

I called Gus and told him what the mystery man said, while Mason was doing the same with Rocco. Gus was going to see what he could find with the info I gave him and get back to us. Afterwards, I called Nate to catch him up on everything and to make sure that all of us were on the same page.

An hour had passed and we had not received any instructions from Gus or Oscar. We discussed the situation among the three of us and came up with our best course of action; well at least for the time being. We let Gus work without any interruptions and positioned ourselves to be ready when we were called. Mason parked close to Brooklyn Bridge Park and we waited. The view was simply beautiful. The sun had disappeared behind the skyscrapers, with darkness about an hour away. The three of us looked out over the East River and enjoyed the view. Although, the reason that we were there was not far from our minds. It was like, "the calm before the storm."

Finally, I received a call. Nate informed me that he and Gus were working together. The time was counting down and all hands needed to be involved in the evolution. Nate had a few matches that met the criteria of the intel that we were given. Gus and the "bomb squad" were not completely sold on the reliability of our source. They were checking on other possibilities, while we went to the locations that Nate had for us. We all were skeptical about the "mystery man," but we had to do something. The three of us were restless from just sitting and waiting, standing on the sidelines is no fun.

The first parking garage we went to was across the bridge on South Street in Manhattan. The "bomb squad" checked out the parking garage on Front Street, which was the only one in Brooklyn that had a view of the bridge. We all came up empty at both locations. They went back to what they were doing and left the rest of the garages to us. They had their own ideas of what we were looking for and kept us out of the loop. I was suspicious of the way everything was being handled on Gus's end. It was like they were running the show and we were just spectators. Now, I was even more curious to learn the identity of the "bomb squad." There had to be a good explanation for Gus to hand us to Nate. Instead of focusing on that, we decided to do what we could with the intel that we received. However, we all felt if they did not use our help, then they had better succeed.

We expeditiously went to the next parking garage on South Street and had the same result. Nevertheless, we continued searching on Pearl Street and then to Cliff Street. We completed the list of garages that we were given and there was no sign of a satellite or any suspicious activity. At this point we were coming up on eight o'clock and the deadline was rapidly approaching. The only option that we had was to revisit the locations, until someone had something better. We believed that Zane's people would wait until the last minute to set up everything to avoid suspicion. It was more wishful thinking than anything.

"Okay, let's hit all of the spots again," Mason said, after we left the parking garage on Cliff Street.

"This is hopeless," Woody stated.

"There's always hope!" I replied.

"Are you guys always this optimistic?" Woody asked.

"Yes we are. This one, more than the rest of us," Mason said, as he pointed at me.

"You have to believe that it'll work out," I stated.

We quickly made our way back over the bridge to Front Street in Brooklyn and began to recheck the parking garages. It felt like time was moving faster; for every second, five had past. It seemed like we were moving in slow motion. It was a little past eight o'clock and our first stop was the Front Street Parking Garage. It was our first time to go there, so there was nothing for us to compare it with. We went around the first level and everything looked normal. The second level was the same, but with only a considerable smaller amount of vehicles. We attempted to go to the third level, but it was blocked off. There was a security patrol truck parked in the way, which immediately raised a red flag. Mason stopped the vehicle and we exited the Yukon to investigate. To that point, there had been no concrete evidence proving that the intel we received was actually true, but all of that was about to change.

While we were looking around the truck with the yellow light on top of it, Nate called and informed us that the "Bomb Squad" had just verified that there were mini-bombs on the Brooklyn Bridge. (My heart started to beat a little faster.) They believed that they had located the vehicle that was used, but they had not taken it down. They had men in position to stop the Governor before he made it to the target area, which was west bound into Manhattan.

"There are mini-bombs on the Brooklyn Bridge, but they haven't been activated yet," I said to Mason and Woody after my phone call had ended.

"I think we may have something. The security camera over there has been disabled," Mason stated.

"How do you know?" Woody asked.

"The wire, in the back of it, has been cut," Mason answered.

"Let's go, we don't have much time. This has to be it!" I said looking at Mason.

"I hope so," Mason replied, as we hurried to the Yukon to get our gear.

"Are you ready for this?" I asked Woody, as I handed him an M-4 assault rifle and Mason gave him a 9mm to use as a back up.

"Do you know how to use that?" Mason asked.

"I went to a gun range once, but that's it. I'll do what I can," Woody replied.

"All we need is for you to have our backs. Here, you'll need this," Mason said, as he gave him a Dragon Skin Vest to put on.

"Stay behind us, keep your head on a swivel, and don't hesitate to pull the trigger. These people are terrorists!" I said to Woody.

"We're not going to interrogate anyone, so feel free to shoot whoever you see," Mason said, while we all were leaving the Yukon. We walked up the ramp and reached the third level. There was no one around in the immediate area. We believed that it was best to explore the area closest to the bridge, which was southwest from where we were. We went in that direction, with the three of us moving quickly and quietly, while bunched together. Up ahead we spotted a man standing in front of the stairway door, talking on a handheld radio that did not resemble a security guard. There was no gun visible, but we assumed that there was one nearby. We got closer and discovered that he was the only person in the area. The man was slowly pacing back and forth in front of the doorway, looking out in the garage, as he held the radio in his left hand that was down by his side. We decided a sneak attack was warranted in that situation, instead of guns blazing. There was a chance the man would tell us what we were up against. We inched closer and waited until his back was to us. When the moment presented itself, we pursued him. Mason was the first to get a hold of him. He wrapped his left arm around the man's throat, spinning him around, all in one motion. He quickly brought his gun up with his right hand and pressed it to the man's head.

"Don't move!" Mason said, as I quickly located his gun that was inside his jacket, while Woody snatched the radio from his hand.

"How many men are on the roof?" I asked.

"I don't know what you are talking about. I'm waiting for my friend," the man replied.

"Why do you have a gun?" I asked.

"This is a very dangerous city at night," he answered.

"He's stalling!" Mason said, as he lowered his gun and moved away from the man.

"Put his hands behind his back and tape his mouth. He's coming with us," I said, as Woody put plexicuffs around the man's wrists and duck tape over his mouth.

"Let's go! The clock's ticking," Mason stated, as he grabbed the man and opened the door to the stairway. We had no idea what to expect on the roof, since we did not have time to interrogate the man. Thus, we were forced to use him as a shield when we opened the door that lead to the roof. We should have threatened him first, to get answers, but there was no time.

We went up the stairs and stopped at the door momentarily, to take a second to gain our composure. Each of us inspected our M-4's and made sure that they were ready to fire. Mason opened the door and followed our hostage onto the roof, staying closely behind him. Woody was the next one out and I was bringing up the rear. We scanned the area as soon as the door opened and the action began in a matter of moments. The lighting on the roof was dim, but you could see the whole area. Within seconds of stepping out of the doorway, I heard a commotion coming from the center of the roof. I caught a glimpse of two men who were looking into a metal case. The light coming from the case made them fairly visible. While moving in their direction, I was looking at a man that was by the west edge of the roof in the direction of Brooklyn Bridge. He had just turned around and raised his gun after his buddies had spotted us. Almost simultaneously, we fired a couple of shots. I dropped the guy that was by the edge of the roof with one of the shots, before he was able to shoot. Mason and Woody fired at the two men by the case, but missed. However, one shot did ricochet off the metal case. We stopped halfway between the case and the door, fanning out in front of the two men. Either they were unprepared or we caught them off guard, because there was no return fire.

"We are unarmed!" One of the men yelled, as we cautiously moved in closer.

"Don't move!" Mason shouted, as he handed our hostage over to Woody, who was standing to his right. A few seconds later, there was a message sent over their radios.

"Arm the bombs!" A voice said over the radios that Woody and the other men had on them. Upon hearing that I immediately felt relieved; we still had time. After hearing the order, Mason and I took a few more steps toward the two men.

"You are too late!" One of the men shouted out, as he threw a handful of objects at us. When they both moved, we opened fire and they immediately fell to the floor. The objects that were thrown were stuck to our guns and one or two made their way back to the metal case.

"It's activated!" Woody shouted, as we ran to the case.

"Fuck! We hesitated too long," Mason said.

"How do you turn it off? We need to stop it!" Woody frantically stated, as we saw that there was a minute and thirty-nine seconds remaining on the timer.

"This is how," I replied, as I pulled a grenade out of my pocket. Mason and Woody did the same. We pulled the pins and tossed the grenades in the metal case and closed it. We took off running, grabbing our hostage on the way, and made it a couple of feet from the door before it exploded.

"Did that stop it?" Woody asked.

"See for yourself," Mason said, as he held his gun out in front of him, displaying that there was no objects attached to it.

"What do we do now?" Woody asked.

"We get the fuck out of here," Mason replied.

"Yeah, someone had to have heard that," I added, as we all went down the stairs to the third level. When we reached the security vehicle, we put the hostage inside and secured his arms to the steering wheel. While walking back to our car, I called Nate and gave him the good news. He was relieved, but this was only half over. At that time, they had nothing, but he was working on it. I called Gus, after hanging up with Nate. I wanted to tell him personally.

"It's done! The case is destroyed and the bombs are deactivated," I said to Gus.

"Oh Kastle, I was worried. It was looking hopeless," Gus stated.

"We need this place cleaned up. Can your boys take care of that?"

"Sure, I'll send them there directly," Gus replied.

"We're on the way to the airport now," I said.

"Okay. How did you do it?" Gus asked.

"We'll discuss it later; just concentrate on stopping the other one. I'll get back to you when we get to the airport," I said.

"Okay, I'll take care of everything. You guys did great," Gus said, as we got in the Yukon. Our conversation ended and we headed out of the parking garage.

"What's the word?" Mason asked.

"We're going to the airport and then to St. Petersburg," I replied, as we exited the garage.

"Do they know anything yet?" Mason asked.

"No," I answered.

"So, we're flying back to Florida? Will we make it in time?" Woody asked.

"We should," I replied.

"You know, I'm feeling pretty good about what I was just apart of. We're heroes," Woody stated.

"We're not done yet," Mason added.

"One down, one to go! Let's get to it!" I stated, feeling very anxious to move on to the next obstacle that we had in front of us.

"What? We can't enjoy this for a few minutes?" Woody replied.

"Yeah, when the mission is complete," Mason said.

"Come on, you two can take a moment to be proud. We just prevented, who knows how many, car bombings," Woody said.

"Look I know you feel good and so do we, but we have one more to stop," I replied, as the 'ice phone' was ringing. I put the call on speaker and answered it. "If you're calling to kiss our ass, it's unnecessary? A simple thank you will do."

"For what…doing the job half-assed? The mission was to stop the bombings and secure the case. This case is destroyed! You should've called the professionals and this would've been a complete success," Oscar stated.

"Why don't you ask Governor Cruz, if this was a success or not," I replied forcefully.

"We had the Governor covered the entire time. He was safe," Oscar retorted.

"We're just glad that we were able to be here to make sure of it. We appreciate your help. Goodbye," I said, as I quickly ended the call.

"Where did Gus find these guys?" Mason stated.

"We'll have to ask him, but you know he'll never tell," I said, as my phone was ringing.

Gus called me to update us on the airport situation. He informed us that all flights would be delayed due to extra security checks and it was possible that we would not be able to leave for hours. There was nothing that we could do, but hope for the best.

Chapter 11
The Skyway

We eagerly waited at the airport for our moment to depart, but we were stuck there. There was no flight, private or commercial, that would get us out of there sooner. It was evident that we were not going to be able to help Rocco and the guys in St. Petersburg. They had to take care of this one without us. Although, Gus assured me that they would have backup. He had a couple of men that were affiliated with the "Bomb Squad" to help out. Gus guaranteed me that the problems we experienced would not happen again and we would have their full cooperation, when it was needed. I had my doubts, but my hands were tied. We agreed to use them, but this time we ran the show. Actually, it was Rocco and Dante who had the reigns. The only involvement in this evolution that Mason and I had was periodical updates from Gus or Nate. We couldn't do anything to stop this and we felt helpless; it was completely up to our friends.

We finally departed at 12:05 A.M., after a three hour wait. According to the intel we had, which had been right on so far, everything would be over before we landed; thus taking the anxiety level to new heights.

At 1:00 A.M., we received an update.

"It's over! I don't have the details yet, but I got the feeling that it didn't go smoothly," Gus informed me.

"Okay, give us a call when you know more," I replied. I immediately phoned Rocco to get the facts.

"I heard you have good news," I said into the speakerphone.

"We did the best we could, but the bombs were set off," Rocco said.

"How bad is it?" Mason asked.

"Just the two vans blew up. No one was killed," Rocco answered.

"How did it go down?" Mason asked.

"Nate discovered that there was an A.P.B. out on a white cargo van for robbing a gas station in St. Petersburg. At the same time they were looking for another white cargo van that had just robbed a gas station five miles south of the Skyway Bridge. After a while, we caught up with the van in St. Petersburg and the "Bomb Squad" found the one that was headed north toward the bridge. We chased the van for miles, going at least ninety miles per hour the entire time. We followed it to the midway point of the bridge and the van slid to a stop, swinging the backend around to where the van blocked most of the road. We saw a guy get out on the drivers side, as we stopped. He started running and then he jumped into the water a few seconds before the van exploded. We went to investigate, but the van across the way in the north bound lane got our attention when it did the same," Rocco stated.

"Was any 'mini-bombs' dropped?" I asked.

"No! Either there were none or they blew up in the vans," Rocco stated.

"So the guys in the vans wanted to be chased?" I said to Rocco.

"Yeah, they did. At both places, they filled the gas tank and then went inside the store. They asked for a plastic bag and stuffed it full of junk food. They stood in line and let the cashier ring up all of it. After the cashier re-bagged everything, they told him to fuck off and left the store," Rocco explained.

"What happened to the drivers?" Mason asked

"They were picked up by the Coast Guard. I sent Gus their names, but I'm sure they're fake," Rocco replied. Later, we found out the names on their fake driver's liscenses were Charley Francis and Ivan Cane.

"Have they talked yet?" I asked.

"Yeah, Dante said that they are telling everything. He and Mo have been out seeing what they could find out. The drivers were hired by Zane Cotto and followed the instructions that he gave them. There was supposed to be a boat waiting for them at the bridge, but it wasn't there. Supposedly, this is the first time they have worked for him," Rocco said.

"This doesn't add up. Until now, Zane didn't want the cops involved. Why does he want to be one of the most wanted men in the world?" I said.

"He's a piece of shit! Who knows why?" Rocco said.

"Maybe he wants to be famous. Then again, there might not be a reason at all," Mason added.

"Oh, there's a reason. Rocco, we'll call you back when we get to Miami," I said.

"Alright, talk to you later," Rocco said, as I ended the call. I phoned Gus again to make sure that Bianca and the others were safe. He assured me that they were now out of danger. He was sure that Zane Cotto was running for his life. The whole country was now looking for him.

After a satisfying conversation with Gus, we informed the pilot to redirect us to Miami and relaxed for the rest of the flight. We all took an overdue power nap, not too long after the phone call ended. We were out like a light.

Chapter 12
The Source

We touched down in Miami at 2:45 A. M. on October 2, 2004. Mason, Woody, and I got off the plane and loaded my Escalade.

"Man, its hot!" Woody shouted. There was an increase in temperature from what we had in New York and on the plane.

"Yeah, it's a little warm," I replied, as I was shedding the black long sleeve shirt that I was wearing. Mason and Woody did the same. Woody had a green t-shirt on underneath, while Mason and I had black shirts. As we all were undressing, my phone rang.

"Hello," I answered, in a voice that sounded like I had a long night and I just woke up.

"Kaz! I've been trying to get in touch with you since yesterday," Rush replied.

"Why? What's going on?" I responded.

"I wanted to see if you and your crew were coming to the concert and the after party. It's still going on. You can stop by," Rush said.

"Maybe another time; it's been a long night," I replied.

"You're missing out," Rush stated.

"Oh, I'm sure!" I said, with a pretty clear picture of what the scene was like there. Rush's parties are always off the hook.

"There's something that you need to know," Rush stated.

"What's that?" I asked.

"When I was at the concert last night, someone sent a letter to my dressing room. It said that someone sent you vital information through a messenger and that person would like to meet with you."

"Where's the meeting place?"

"I'm instructed to give you a phone number. I'll send it to your phone when we hang up. Look, I don't know anything about this and I don't want to know. I've learned my lesson!"

"That's good to hear."

"I'm going to keep my nose clean and enjoy my life that I'm fortunate to have; thanks to you. I don't know how you pulled it off, but I owe you. I am free! I love you man!" While Rush was talking, I could tell that he was boozed up. He was, definitely, enjoying his freedom.

"You're welcome and thanks for the number," I replied.

"You got it! Look, I want to do something nice for you soon," Rush stated.

"Okay, we'll get together in the coming weeks. I'll be in touch," I said.

"Take it easy, bro," Rush replied, as we both hung up. I called Nate and he informed me that the others were on their way back. We all got in the vehicle and Mason drove us from Kendall Airport. I dialed the number that Rush gave me on the way home. The unrecognizable voice informed me that the meeting would take place ten miles north at Opa Locka Airport, which is the same size as Kendall. We just used Kendall Airport, because it was the closest to our houses.

We arrived at the location as directed and found a black cargo van near a private jet. We parked beside the van and exited our vehicle. Woody, hidden by the tinted windows and darkness, stayed inside the Escalade. The three of us thought it was best for him to stay there, until we found out who we were dealing with. Mason and I were escorted to a black Cadillac Deville by three men that were wearing black coats. They had concealed weapons, as did we. I was patted down and forced to relinquish my 9mm, before I was allowed to meet the mystery man. I agreed to hand it over to Mason, which sufficed.

"Are you sure about this?" Mason asked, as he glanced over at me

"Yes. I have to know who's in there," I replied. The door was opened for me and I walked to it. I took a few steps and saw a man's shoes, then his leg before I fully got in the car. I closed the door, once I was all the way in. I stared at the mystery man the entire time. I had never seen him before in my life, but the scar underneath his lip gave me a good idea to who he was.

"Kastle Raines, it's a pleasure to meet you," the man said, with a Spanish accent, as he shook my hand. "My name is Esteban Ortiz."

"Your name sounds familiar," I cautiously responded.

"My name has probably come up recently in connection with my ex-business associate, Zane Cotto," Esteban stated. Esteban's empire is spread all over South America, but his home base is in Mexico. The Ortiz Cartel is one of many, but his is the biggest. He has the power.

"I heard that you two are partners. So, you can understand my surprise, when I see that it's you who sold him out."

"I use a number of smugglers to get my product into the states. He's the biggest one on the east coast and our names are often intertwined."

"So, the shipment that was taken down Thursday morning wasn't his?" I asked, as I began to piece everything together.

"No it wasn't. He leaked its arrival to provide an aversion, so his load of explosives would arrive without any problems. The money that was lost is unacceptable. I got a hold of some of his men and discovered what he had planned. He believes that bombings make everyone want to get high."

"Did you know about any bombings in the past?"

"No! Killing potential consumers is bad business and stupid. I want all Americans to buy my product and enjoy their lives. I knew if the bombings were successful then your government would come after me with everything they have, especially with an assassination of a Presidential Candidate. I sent word to you, so it would be stopped. I thank you."

"It was our pleasure. The intel was really helpful. We thank you. We did everything we could to stop the bombing in Florida," I stated.

"I know. When he failed in New York, he had to blow up something. It wasn't about killing people anymore. He plans to get caught and blame it all on me. He'll tell them everything they want to hear," Esteban explained.

"I knew that something had to be going on for it to happen like that," I replied.

"He has been planning this for a while. He came to me with his bomb that he created and I told him that I wanted nothing to do with car bombs. I admit that it is a good idea, but it's not something I want to be involved with. He's a brilliant man. If only he used it in different ways," Esteban said.

"What about your messengers? Why use Sammy and Rush?" I asked him, in an attempt to piece everything together.

"I heard from different people that Zane was up to something. The more I looked into it, your name came up. After I figured out Zane's plan, I needed someone you knew to get information to you. When my shipment was busted, you were seen talking with the black guy. I used him at first. I had you checked out and found that you did security for Rushon Little. I thought you would be more likely to meet with me if it came from him," Esteban explained.

"Didn't you go and see Rush at his house?" I asked.

"Zane brought me there a few months ago, to speak to someone about transporting his bombs that he was making. That's when I first heard about his plan. Once we got there, Rushon Little didn't even know who he was and he never said anything about transporting bombs. He wanted us to be seen together, so he could say I was behind it all. It was all part of his plan. Thanks to you, it didn't work," Esteban said.

"It's good to have allies in time of need," I replied.

"Yes it is. If you ever need me to return the favor, don't hesitate to ask. I'm in debt to you," Esteban stated.

"I'll keep you in mind," I replied.

"I want you to know that you don't have to worry about Zane Cotto ever again. His ass is mine. It's only a matter of time before my men find him and he will pay for what he has done," Esteban said.

"Thank you," I responded.

"We probably will never see each other again. Various U.S. agencies do not like me too much," Esteban stated.

"Nevertheless, it was a pleasure. I'm glad that I had the chance to meet you," I replied, as we shook hands again. I opened the door and got out of the car. While Mason and I were walking to the Escalade, I revealed that Esteban was the source. We decided to keep that close to the vest, until we were behind closed doors with Rocco and Dante.

We left the airport and I told them about my conversation with the source.

"Does that mean that this is over?" Woody asked.

"Yeah, Zane is running from half of Mexico as we speak," I answered.

"I want to thank you two for everything. The past few days have given me something I can really be proud of," Woody said.

"You were a little slow in the beginning, but you came through for us. You really helped out," Mason said to Woody.

"I'm glad I was able to do so," Woody replied. I called Gus to pass along what I had learned and he gave me an update. He wanted to know the identity of the source, but I wouldn't give it to him. I wanted to know who the bomb squad was before I told him anything. He would not budge, so neither did I. The main thing is that he was informed of the important stuff. He told me that he would be going to see his wife after a while and may not be there when we all arrived. I thanked Gus for his help and we made plans to get together before they went back to Jacksonville or to Paris. He was not sure where they would be going.

I called Nate and we all discussed the remaining tasks that had to be done for this day to be over. We decided that Mason would drop me off at the office, since it was close by, and he would take Woody anywhere he needed to go. Nate was going to pick me up, after he took Lindsay to her car; she was free to go home. Before I got off the phone, Nate had a few things to tell me. I had asked him to find out something a few days before and he now had answers for me. He was very persistent. I thanked him for his hard work and we planned to discuss it when he came to get me.

Upon arrival, Mason, Woody, and I unloaded all of our gear and put it in the small storage building, located behind the office. We didn't want to have an arsenal with them, while they were driving out of town. If they were stopped, there was no way to explain all of that. We had good luck with the authorities up to that point, so why push our luck when we did not need to.

Before Mason and Woody departed, I had something for us to talk about.

"Woody, it's been a pleasure, but I wish you would've trusted us. You could have told us your real name," I said.

"What are you talking about?" Mason asked.

"His name is Jerry Walsh. He's an FBI Agent," I replied, as the two of us stared at Woody. A couple of seconds went by and nothing was said. Woody did not move an inch. He looked scared for his life.

"I like Woody better," Mason stated, breaking the silence.

After he took a deep breath, Woody spoke. "How did you find out?"

"Nate discovered that an Agent Walsh tipped off the FBI Field Office in Tampa of two vans loaded with explosives going over the Skyway Bridge. He checked him out and found his picture. Also, it seems our friend here has his own retirement fund set aside, courtesy of Zane Cotto.

You have a few accounts other than the one in your shoe," I explained.

"I work at a desk. I've been there for eight years and I'm nowhere. When I was on vacation a while back, I first got involved with the Cottos. I created Greg Carpenter on my own. The plan was to get all the evidence I could and give it to my superiors to move up the ladder. I did keep some money in an offshore account. I was doing this with no backup. I felt I should be rewarded for my trouble," Woody stated.

"When did you call in the tip?" Mason asked.

"While we were waiting at the airport," Woody answered.

"So, where do we stand with you?" I asked.

"I've never met you guys. The things I've seen will stay with me until I die," Woody replied.

"I don't know. It might be hard for an ambitions man like yourself to do that," I responded.

"When you're debriefed, you might crack and spill everything," Mason added.

"Mason's right. Do you have a cover story?" I asked.

"I'm on vacation this week. I go back to work on Monday. I'll say I was in New York sightseeing, when I received a tip from a source," Woody said.

"We can help with that. You'll need hotel receipts, plane tickets, and other stuff to back it up," I stated, as Woody exhaled.

"You're right. Why would you do that?" Woody replied.

"It's always good to know people in high places," I said.

"I'm still on the bottom floor," Woody responded.

"Well it's time that we get you in the penthouse," Mason said.

"As long as we help each other, we'll make it happen. Are we in agreement?" I asked.

"Yes we are," Woody said with a smile.

"We will start by showing you how to hide your other money better," I stated.

"We can't have a friend of ours labeled as a corrupt agent. This is going to be good. We won't have to break the law. We can pass along everything that we hear to you," Mason added.

"I have a feeling that this is the beginning of a great relationship," Woody said, as he stuck out his right hand to seal our alliance.

"I think so," I replied, as Mason and I shook his hand. We said our goodbyes and he went to the car, while Mason hung back with me.

"This could not have worked out any better. We now have a federal agent on our side," Mason said.

"He needs to have more power. We'll have to build him up and then he can be useful," I replied.

"Yeah. I'm just glad that it went down like this. I didn't want to kill him," Mason said.

"I don't know where this is going, but I want to be prepared. We need to surround ourselves with people we trust, like Nate," I stated.

"I think we can trust Woody," Mason replied.

"Take him under your wing and feel him out," I said. The more I thought about it, I was excited with the new element Woody would bring. We could distance ourselves from danger and accomplish our objectives.

"What about Mo?" Mason asked.

"I'm still undecided. We will talk about it when we get together tomorrow," I said.

"We'll have a celebratory smoke," Mason stated.

"I know a guy," I replied, as we both smiled.

"Let me get Special Agent Woody home. I'll see you tomorrow," Mason said.

"See ya," I said, as Mason walked off and took Woody to Juno Beach; while, I stayed behind and waited for Nate to arrive.

Chapter 13
A. D.

I watched Mason drive off and then walked to the front of the security firm building. I unlocked the front door and went inside, locking the door behind me. I turned on most of the lights, upon entering. I walked through the small waiting area and continued to an open area that had six desks spread around the room. In the very back, there were two rooms. Rocco's office was the room on the right and my office was on the left. There were three exits: the front door and each of the offices had a backdoor. I walked in my office, turned on the light and sat at my desk. I had time to kill, so I checked my email and messed around on the computer. It had been over a week, since I had checked it. While I was keying in my password, "k5brain," my phone rang.

"Nate! Where are you?"

"I just dropped Lindsay off at her car. I should be there in about twenty minutes."

"Okay, park in the back. There are a few things that we have to get out of storage."

"Alright, I'll be there shortly. Kastle, I need to tell you something," Nate said.

"Okay," I replied.

"While I was in your safe, I was nosey. I found a letter that was entitled 'Operation K5.' I read some of it, before I put it back in. There was something about the texture of the paper that felt weird to me. I put it under a black light and saw wings. I did a search and found that it's similar to Air Force Pilot's Wings," Nate explained.

"Interesting," I said.

"Do you know why it was there?" Nate asked.

"I have no idea," I responded.

"I just thought it was odd that it was hidden. I didn't have much time to research it, but that will give me something to do tomorrow," Nate said.

"It can wait. You can take a few days off; you deserve it. You can have a week, if you want," I stated.

"I may take you up on that. I'll see you in a little while," Nate said, as we hung up.

After I finished with my email, I started looking for news reports of the night's events. I searched for reports from national and local outlets in New York and St. Petersburg. While doing so, I heard a noise coming from outside of my office. I grabbed my 9mm and walked, little by little, toward the doorway, scanning the room as much as I could. I held my pistol down by my side, as I quietly stepped out of my office and saw an empty room. I walked to my left and made my way to Rocco's office door. I turned the knob slowly and gradually eased the door open, while slowly raising my gun. As the door was opening, I heard a voice. "Don't shoot!" I immediately stopped moving the door. I reached my hand in and flipped the light switch. I pushed the door open and pointed my gun all in one motion. "I'm unarmed!"

"This day couldn't get any better," I said, as I cracked a huge smile.

"Well done! I don't know how you did it?" Zane Cotto said, as he sat behind the desk. There are no words to express how happy I was at that moment.

"Stand up and keep your hands where I can see them!" I said, while my gun was continuously aimed at him.

"Okay," he replied, as he put his hands up and backed the rolling chair out away from the desk. He stood up and took a few steps in my direction before stopping.

"So, this is my reward for playing your little game," I said.

"The game's over and you were the victor, but you won't get what you want. So, in the end, I am the real winner," Zane replied.

"Stop your babbling about games and real winners. I don't want to hear anything from you. There's nothing that you could say that would exonerate you for what you've done. You're dead!"

"No I'm not, I'm here to turn myself in and you're going to take me there," Zane replied, with a grin.

"I'm going to take you somewhere alright...to the bottom of the ocean floor. You won't be alone...the Cotto family plot is down there," I said.

"There are laws about killing an unarmed man in your country. There's no proof that I've done anything wrong. I'll go and give your government everything to bring down the Ortiz Drug Empire. I have evidence that will make that happen. I'll say that I made the bombs for Esteban and I carried out his orders. I'll walk away and live a long life in this country. Am I smart or what? Everything went as planned. The little evidence that does exist, leads to an innocent man. Every person that was used in this, met with Esteban. They were made to believe that the orders were made by him," Zane said, as he continued grinning.

"I have my own laws that you've broken and there's only one punishment that fits the crime. I'm going to put a grenade in your mouth and pull the pin…an eye for an eye motherfucker!" I said forcefully, with a serious look on my face.

"You're bluffing," Zane replied.

"Not this time," I said.

"You have a son on the way; I know you want to see him grow up. I'm here as a customer. I need protection from an international drug lord who's going to kill me," Zane said.

"He's not going to kill you, but he'll win in the end," I replied, as my finger was touching the trigger.

"Your country needs me. They need to know how my bombs are made and I'm the only one that can do that. I thought about selling the blueprint to the highest bidding terrorist group, but I decided that it would be fun to work for the U.S. Government."

"You may want the American dream like your brother, but it'll never happen," I replied.

"It will…and you're going to be forced to watch," Zane responded, as he smiled and even winked at me.

"Oh, you're dead," I proclaimed.

"Face it! You're not going to pull the trigger. You have a normal life again. You won't throw that away. This is over," Zane stated.

"It is over," I responded.

"Kastle! Wait!" A voice screamed from outside of the room.

"You're late! He was about to kill me," Zane said.

"Shut the fuck up!" The voice replied, as it got closer and closer until a man appeared in the doorway. I stood there completely and utterly shocked from who I saw.

"Banks!"

"Kastle, my boy! It's great to see you," Banks replied, while I remained stunned.

"You're Banks Newman!" Zane stated, looking very surprised.

"Why are you here?" I asked Banks.

"I need to bring him with me," he answered.

"He's not going with anyone, not even you," I replied.

"He has to. I would love to see him get what he deserves, but it's not up to me and you. There's a bigger picture that supersedes everything."

"What would that be?" I said, as I continued to point my gun at Zane.

"Look, I'm ready to go. If you want my help, get me out of here. Now!" Zane said.

"You have nowhere to go. Everyone wants you dead. If you want to live, keep your mouth shut," Banks replied.

"Start from the beginning. I want to know why I went to your funeral," I stated.

"Have you ever heard of the 'Angels of Defense'?" Banks asked.

"I have… So, it's not a myth," I replied.

"Are you really going to tell a story right now?" Zane asked.

"I will kill you myself, if you speak again," Banks said, as he stared at Zane.

"Okay! Can he at least lower the gun?" Zane asked.

"No!" I emphatically responded.

"In the late seventies and early eighties, there were many terrorist attacks and even more plots against the United States. In New York, there were three multimillionaires that had too much free time on their hands and felt that it was their duty as Americans to do something to help out. They found that they could get useful information, given that they were not associated with government in any way. They loved the lives that they had and didn't want their identities to be known. Any crucial information that they came across, they gave it to the President."

"How did they do that?" I asked.

"They would send a letter to someone on the White House kitchen staff. The President would have each letter traced, but no one was able to find out where the letters were coming from. They began to accumulate contacts and had a steady dose of information for the President for a couple of years. The three men were getting older and wanted to make sure what they had created would live on. So, they began to search for men to keep everything going for years to come and to meet with the President face to face. This was mainly because of the 'gunshot' incident. In '81, they sent the President information on an assassination plot, but apparently he did not receive it or his people did not believe it. The three men had many candidates, but they only found one that met the standard that they were looking for. One of their sources tipped them off about an escaped POW. The man was an Air Force pilot that crashed his plane and was pronounced dead. He was taken prisoner and tortured for two years, before he escaped. He told no one that he was alive and went straight home to see his wife and two year old child. He discovered that his wife had remarried and had a new life. After revealing everything the three men had done for the previous seven years, they persuaded the ex-pilot to carry out their creation. He went through hell when he was captured and he didn't want anyone to ever experience that, so he accepted their offer. You know it must have been devastating for him to let his family believe that he was dead. Although, he does monitor their lives and makes sure that they are safe. The three men gave him total control and he vowed to never let their identities be known. In 1988, a few months before the President left office, the man met with the President of the

United States face to face. He explained everything to the President and they came to an agreement to continue the secret alliance. They believed it was best for the future of this country. The man was passed along from President to President. Roman was a powerful man; he had the President's ear at his disposal. He began to recruit other men, but to join they could not exist."

"Like someone who died in a plane crash," I added, which made Banks smile.

"Yes. He looked for men who had nothing and loved this country. Over the years, with all of the technology and manpower, the group primarily carried out the President's wishes. Since they don't exist, they can do things that will not lead back to him."

"How long have you been apart of this?" I inquired.

"I have been a contact of Roman's for years. The plan was for me to join after my daughter had a husband to take care of her. On the day of the school bombing in Jacksonville my plans had to be altered. I didn't meet him, until after the plane crash," Banks stated.

"So, everything that we were involved with in the past was associated with the 'Angels of Defense'?" I said.

"People who don't exist cannot be seen. They provide, handpicked, capable personnel, the means to get what they want done. Yes, we used the security firm to get information on the Cotto Organization and put it in the right hands."

"Can we go now?" Zane asked, but we gave him no response. I wanted more answers.

"Why are you showing your face and why in the fuck are you here for him?" I asked.

"President Russell wants Esteban Ortiz and he can give him to us. I knew you guys would eventually find him, so I made this meeting happen. The only way I could keep him alive is to come here and explain everything to you. I wanted you to know the importance of the situation," Banks replied.

"So, it doesn't matter what he's done. The President believes that it may get him re-elected." I stated.

"Whatever the reason, there is no denying that Esteban is no saint. You guys did good today; I'm proud. How did you find out about the targets?" Banks asked.

"That's what I want to know?" Zane added.

"I thought Gus got it from you," I answered.

"No, it didn't come from us," Banks responded.

"But you're his source, are you not?" I asked.

"We are, but he doesn't know who it's coming from. He doesn't know I'm alive," Banks informed me.

"You know we could've used a little heads up that all of this was about to happen," I said.

"You guys did great by yourselves. We didn't know anything about this, until Roman's daughter didn't go home one night and her phone was turned off. He wanted me to be sure and thank you."

"Wow! It's a small world. You can tell Mr. Clark that it was our pleasure. He's going to be jealous when he finds out that you had the pleasure of watching the man, who put his daughter in danger, die," I stated.

"You still didn't answer the question. Who helped you?" Zane asked.

"I'm not at liberty to say," I responded.

"In our country, we don't give up our sources," Banks said to Zane.

"I'm tired of that gun being pointed at me. Drop the gun or the deal is off!" Zane shouted.

"If you don't make a deal, then you're all his. You'll have a long and painful death," Banks explained.

"I'm not dropping anything!" I said looking Zane in his eyes.

"Lower your gun!" Banks said.

"He's not walking away from this. I want this to be over, it's the only way," I responded

"This will never be over. There are wars fought everyday. Some are small and some are big. Sometimes you have to do things for the country that you don't agree with, but it's for the greater good. If the bombings in New York were successful, then I wouldn't be here and he wouldn't have a deal. The American people will never know what happened last night and they will continue to feel safe. Our work is never known," Banks said.

"Aren't you afraid of your identities ever being revealed?" I asked.

"There are many secrets that each President must take to the grave and this is one of them. They understand the significance of the code and appreciate our contributions. They believe our existence is necessary and it has been proven over and over again."

"Are the stories over with now? Can we go?" Zane stated, as I turned and acknowledged him.

"It's over," I said, as I aimed at his head and pulled the trigger. Blood splattered on the wall, as he fell to the floor. One shot to his forehead is all it took. Zane Cotto was dead!

"I didn't think you would ever do it. What made you go through with it?"

"You're not mad?" I was expecting Banks to be upset.

"No! I was good either way. The President doesn't always get what he wants, although we honestly do try to grant his wishes. This time I was a little late in getting to the location where the mark was at."

"You threw me for a second, but I knew that you wouldn't be telling your secrets if you wanted him to live. Truthfully, he was dead when I saw him. There was no way that I was going to be talked out of doing it."

"We could've had it done, but we wanted you to have the honor; a little thank you for the week that all of you had to endure."

"So, this is about politics?"

"What do you mean?"

"Since your organization does what the President wants, then he must not be the popular choice for the next four years. The President wanted the bombings stopped in New York to prevent Governor Cruz from getting sympathy votes. He wants Esteban Ortiz to have a better chance to win the election, but that won't happen now. Power does have its advantages, doesn't it?"

"You're a fast learner. So, what do you say?"

"What?"

"You knew that I would eventually ask you and the guys to be the team I use when something needs to be done. You would continue living your life, nothing would change. When something comes up, I would call you guys to take care of it. You would be enforcers."

"Were the guys in New York part of your team?"

"No, but they're somebody's."

"We were not impressed. You could use an upgrade, but I'll have to think about it. I'll run it by the guys and let them make their own decision, but for me, everything is different now. Let me think about?"

"You'll realize that this is for you. If it wasn't, than you wouldn't be standing here carrying on a conversation with a corpse at your feet. In your eyes, he's not here. Most people would be trying to get out of Dodge," Banks replied, as he glanced down at Zane Cotto's body.

"I'm still here, because there are a few things that I'm curious about."

"Like what?"

"I have to know about Adam."

"What do you want to know?"

"Did he know about all of this? Was he doing what he was told and we killed him."

"You know what the rules are. He started working with the Cottos behind our backs. When they went after him, he got scared and gave them up; but it was too late. You guys had no choice. He forced your hand."

"What about in the beginning?"

"We got involved with the Cottos, so we could see what they were up to. Once we got what we needed from them, Adam was supposed to cut all ties with them, but he didn't."

"What did you get from them?"

"Adam and Ponce became close. Ponce wanted to be free of his brothers and have a life in America. Adam brought him to me and told him that I could make it happen. Ponce was going to give us information to put the Cottos out of business, but the higher ups wanted Esteban Ortiz. The only way to get him was through Zane. That wasn't going to happen, so I told him that I couldn't help him. After that, Adam and Ponce weren't happy with me," Banks said.

"What was the information that he wanted to give you?" I asked.

"A list of the Cottos' bank account numbers that held all of their money. They could've been wiped out."

"So, what happened?"

"The school bombing happened. Then, the Cottos began disappearing, so there was no need to use it."

"Are you saying that you could have prevented all of this from happening today?"

"It may have been harder for him to do this without his money, but he had other resources to go to. It would've happened regardless."

"You know I've had that piece of paper that you left behind all of this time and I didn't know what was on it until today," I said, referring to Nate's discovery.

"I knew you would find it one day," Banks replied.

"Actually, it wasn't me. Nate did," I stated.

"Yeah, I see that you're doing what a good leader should do. Surround yourself with smart and trustworthy people. Everything is now in place. All you have to do is complete the mission that the team is given, when you're called upon. This has been my plan all along. All you have to do is say yes and you'll be an essential part of something special."

"What if I don't want that?"

"You wouldn't be called everyday, maybe not even every year. You guys would only handle the important stuff," Banks said, as he continued to sell me on the idea.

"So you're like the kings of the intelligence underworld and we would be your enforcers?" I stated.

"We ARE the intelligence underworld," Banks responded.

"It's tempting, but I'll have to talk it over with the guys," I replied.

"Take all the time that you need."

"Okay, I will. It's great to see you, you look good. I know you enjoy all of this, it definitely fits you. What's the protocol, if someone knows your existence?"

"Nothing, if the person has the same beliefs as I do. I trust you. Can you guys clean this up?"

"Yeah, we've done this before."

"Well, it was good seeing you. I'll be checking up on you guys from time to time," Banks stated.

"How is Sarah doing?" I asked.

"She's great. I watch over her as well."

"So, she doesn't know?"

"No! She has a second chance at happiness and that's all I ever hoped for her," Banks said, while my phone began to ring. I looked at the Caller ID and saw a strange number.

"Hello," I said, answering the call.

"Kastle! The babies are coming! Isabella is bringing me to the hospital now!" Bianca shouted.

"I'm in Miami! I'm on the way. I love you, baby!" I replied.

"I love you too. Hurry!" She screamed; I assumed it was during a contraction. "It shouldn't be too much longer," Isabella said quickly, but in a calmer voice.

"Okay! I'll see you there," I replied, before we hung up.

"I have to get to the hospital. Bianca is about to have the babies," I said to Banks.

"Babies?"

"A boy and a girl," I said with pride.

"Congratulations! I'll get this taken care of. I can have a team here in fifteen minutes. They'll make this place spotless. There will be no DNA, no gunshot residue, and no body. I can't be here, but it'll be done."

"Are you sure?"

"Yes, get to the hospital. You don't need to miss your children's birth," Banks said.

"Okay! I'll leave that door unlocked. Thank you," I said, as I shook his hand.

"I'll see you soon. Get to the hospital!" Banks said.

"See ya!" I replied, as we exited the office. Banks went out of the back door and I headed to the front. I stopped near the midway point and turned around. I remembered Zane stating that he had evidence on Esteban, so it could possibly be with him. I thought about doing it earlier, but I was distracted by Banks and his bombshells. I returned to his body that was lying on the floor. I inspected both of his arms, but there was no visible marks to make me believe that there could be something hidden, like a microchip. I searched his pockets and found a flash drive in the left front pocket. I knew then that I needed some sleep, if I was checking for microchips underneath the skin before I had searched his pockets. I took the flash drive and rapidly went toward the front. I quickly turned out the lights on my way out the door. While I was locking up, I dialed Nate and put the phone up to my ear.

"Where are you? Bianca is having the babies. I need to get to the hospital," I said in to the phone, talking very fast.

"I'll be there soon! I'm a few minutes out," Nate responded.

"Please hurry! I'll be waiting on the curb and..." The conversation was interrupted, by a gunshot that rang out, and subsequently ended; while the cell phone lay on the sidewalk, with blood not too far away.

Chapter 14
Hail Mary

"Oh Bianca, they are so precious!" Sophie said, once she made it next to Bianca's hospital bed. She and Tristan had flown in from New York and had just arrived at the hospital. Sophie handed Bianca a gift bag that consisted of two baby blankets: one blue and one pink.

"They are adorable! Where's the father at? I've been calling, for the past two hours," Tristan said, as Isabella, Rocco, and Mason walked into the room.

"That's what I want to know! I'm going to kill him. Isabella has called him all morning and he was on his way each time," Bianca said.

"Where is he?" Sophie asked, as there was a moment of silence.

"Sweetie, I didn't call him. I didn't want to give you stress," Isabella replied.

"We did what was best for you and the babies," Rocco said, as he intervened.

"What are you talking about? You're scaring me!" Bianca said.

"Rocco, what's going on?" Tristan asked.

"He was shot this morning," Mason said.

"What? I talked to him this morning," Bianca responded.

"All we can figure, that it happen sometime after that. He's in surgery now," Rocco stated.

"I want to see him!" Bianca said, as her eyes were tearing up.

"There's nothing you can do for him now. We'll get them to let us know when he's out of surgery. Then, we'll do whatever is necessary to get you in there to see him," Rocco said. A few minutes later, the guys exited the room. While they were in the hallway talking, a nurse walked by them.

"Excuse me! Mrs. Jennings," Tristan said, as he stopped her and read her name tag.

"Yes!" she replied.

"Can you find out for me if a patient here is out of surgery?" Tristan said to the nurse, who, obviously, recognized who he was.

"Yes I can! What's his name?" She asked.

"Kastle Raines. He was brought in for a gunshot wound," Tristan explained.

"Sure thing! I'll come back personally, as soon as I locate him," she said.

"Thank you so much!" Tristan said, as she walked away. "Does anyone know how this happened?" Tristan asked the guys, as they stood out in the hallway.

"No, but we'll find out," Rocco responded.

"Have you guys seen him yet?" Tristan asked.

"No, we were out of town on business. We arrived here a few minutes after you," Mason replied.

"Isabella has been keeping us posted on his condition. I can't believe that this has happened," Rocco said.

"Kastle is tuff. He'll be okay," Mason stated, as the nurse was approaching Tristan.

"He's a fighter," Rocco added.

"Where's Dante?" Mason asked.

"He and Mo stayed behind to look into something," Rocco explained. They discovered that the F.B.I. received a tip before the bombs exploded and they were trying to find out who that person was.

"Mr. Lake, I'm sorry to inform you that Mr. Raines didn't make it. The surgeon is on his way up to speak to the family. I'm truly sorry," she said, as a genuine look of sadness became visible on Tristan's face. Rocco was teary-eyed and they all were totally shocked.

"Thank you, but I think that it's best if it comes from us. This is going to be hard," Rocco stated.

"I'll do it," Tristan said, as Rocco's phone started to ring.

"I'm going to take this. Go ahead without me," Rocco said, as the guys walked in the room and he answered the call. "Where the fuck are you?"

"I've been at the police station for the past two hours," Nate replied, while Rocco was hearing a large amount of crying coming from the room.

"Why?" Rocco asked.

"When I arrived at the office, Kastle had already been shot. The ambulance arrived there moments after I did. A cop asked me a few questions, while they were investigating the area. They found, the back door to your office had been broken into and, Zane Cotto lying dead on the floor," Nate explained.

"What?"

"They matched the bullet to the gun that Kastle had on him. It was confirmed that Kastle shot him at point-blank range; but, they haven't identified the body and I didn't tell help them out. He didn't have an I.D. and his prints aren't in the system. They know Zane was unarmed and there were no signs of a struggle. They're throwing out words like, execution-style murder. They're waiting for Kastle to get out of surgery to question him and they want to talk to you as well. I didn't tell them about anything that has happened this week or about anyone I've met. They grilled me for two hours, but I didn't give them anything," Nate informed Rocco.

"Kastle didn't make it through surgery. He's dead," Rocco stated.

"Oh my God!"

"I know! You can think about Kastle later, we have to cover our asses. They should be getting warrants as we speak. Go and erase any incriminating evidence that you may have. Go to Kastle's and do the same."

"It's already done."

"Do they know who shot him?" Rocco asked.

"No! The detective that questioned me said he was shot from long range. They haven't found the bullet or the gun yet," Nate said.

"I want you to check all surveillance cameras in the area as soon as possible," Rocco ordered.

"I will. There's something that you need to know."

"What?"

"Kastle gave me something seconds before the ambulance got there. He gave me a flash drive that he got off of Zane. I just got a chance to check it out. It contains a list of offshore account numbers. I've only looked in three of the accounts so far, and there are seven figures in each of them. There has to be at least thirty accounts on the list." Nate explained.

"Bring it to me. We all need to sit down and go over what has happened in the last three hours." Rocco said, as Isabella walked out of the room.

"Okay, I'm on the way," Nate said, as he and Rocco hung up. Isabella came up to Rocco and he gave her a comforting hug, while she was crying.

"What are you going to do?" Isabella asked, as she let go of Rocco and took a step back.

"You already know!"

"Look at Bianca in there. That's what I will look like, if you guys won't stop all of this. Talk to whomever that you need to and tell them everything that you know and be done with it," Isabella replied.

"It's not that simple; I can't just step aside and do nothing. I'm not made that way."

"Sure you can; for your family you will," Isabella responded.

"I lost my brother today. He was family," Rocco said.

"You need to let the cops do their job."

"That's not an option."

"Don't you think the person, who did this, will come after one of you next?"

"We are going after him! We won't stop, until we find the piece of shit."

"There is no talking you out of this, is it?"

"No! It's who I am," Rocco said, which produced a couple seconds of silence.

"Okay! If you must go through with it, I want you to find this person and make their body disappear. Do whatever you have to do. I cannot lose you," Isabella responded, as she and Rocco hugged again.

"Consider it done!" Rocco replied, as Isabella returned to the room. Mason joined Rocco at the door and they went in the hallway.

"Who was on the phone earlier?" Mason asked, as the three of them stood in a circle out in the hall.

"That was Nate. Zane Cotto was shot and killed in my office, just minutes before Kastle was shot on the sidewalk from long range. Nate's on the way here, so we can piece all of this together," Rocco stated.

"Do the cops have any leads?" Mason asked.

"No," Rocco replied, as Tristan walked passed them.

"Where're you going?" Mason asked.

"I'm going to go and say goodbye to my friend," Tristan replied.

"Hold up! We'll go with you," Mason said. Tristan, Rocco, and Mason made their way to the elevators. The elevator ride was quiet. Each one of them were preparing themselves for what they were about to see. They walked down the hall and came to the nurses' station, where they were met by Mary.

"Hello. Can you tell us what room Kastle Raines is in?" Rocco asked Mrs. Jennings.

"We just want to say our goodbyes. Can you sneak us in?" Tristan said.

"We won't be long," Mason added.

"Okay. It's down the hall, third door on the right," the nurse replied.

"Thank you. We appreciate it," Tristan replied. The three of them walked in the room and closed the door behind them. They were true to their word and only stayed for a few minutes.

The door opened and Tristan, Rocco, and Mason walked out of the room. They stopped in the middle of the hallway and began talking.

"The cops are going to want to question me. I'm going to go ahead and get that out of the way," Rocco stated.

"I'm headed back to the room," Tristan said.

"I'll see you up there," Rocco replied, as Tristan walked off. "You need to meet up with Nate and see what he knows. If you are around when the cops get here, then you'll be stuck answering questions all day," Rocco said.

"I don't want that. I'm out," Mason replied, as he walked away. Rocco stood there for a moment and processed what he had just seen, before he walked to the elevators. On the way, he saw Mrs. Jennings walking toward him.

"Excuse me, Mrs. Jennings?" Rocco said, as he stood in front of the nurses.

"Please, call me Mary," she answered, as the other nurses walked on.

"You look familiar. Do you have a daughter that works at the Overlay Restaurant?" Rocco asked.

"Yes, I do. She works there part time, while she's in nursing school," Mary replied.

"You two look a lot alike. I've been there many times over the past six months. You've raised a wonderful young woman," Rocco said.

"My daughter and I have a special relationship. We're like best friends. I talk to Becky everyday," Mary stated.

"I thought so. Well, I'll let you get back to work," Rocco said.

"Yeah, it has been a busy morning," Mary replied.

"Were there anymore gunshot victims this morning?" Rocco asked.

"Yes, there was another one that came in at about the same time. A gunshot wound to the shoulder," Mary answered.

"What's his name?" Rocco asked.

"Felix Santana," Mary responded.

"Where's his room?" Rocco asked.

"He disappeared from his room, not too long after his surgery. I guess he didn't want to stick around and have to answer any questions. He was lucky. If the bullet would've been a few inches down, he would've died. I guess one angel got his wings today... It's too bad that your friend wasn't as fortunate," Mary stated.

"Yeah, it's too bad. You've been very helpful. Thank you," Rocco said.

"You're welcome. I'm sorry for your loss," Mary replied.

"Thank you," Rocco said. Then, they went their separate ways.